Christmas in Paradise

by

Kathi Daley

D1523730

This book is a work of fiction. Names, characters, places, and incidents either are products of the author's imagination or are used fictitiously. Any resemblance to actual events or locales or persons, living or dead, is entirely coincidental.

This book is dedicated to my son Danny, who will be graduating from the University of Edinburgh with his master's degree at about the same time this book comes out. Congratulations, Danny. I love you and am proud of you.

I also want to thank the very talented Jessica Fischer for the cover art.

And I must mention my team of advance readers for taking time out of their busy lives to help me launch each new book and the awesome bloggers in my life for helping me publicize them.

And, as always, love and thanks to my sister Christy for her time, encouragement, and unwavering support. I also want to thank Carrie, Cristin, Brennen, and Danny for the Facebook shares, Randy Ladenheim-Gil for the editing, and, last but not least, my super-husband Ken for allowing me time to write by taking care of everything else.

Books by Kathi Daley

Paradise Lake Series:
Pumpkins in Paradise
Snowmen in Paradise
Bikinis in Paradise
Christmas in Paradise
Puppies in Paradise – February 2015

Zoe Donovan Mysteries:
Halloween Hijinks
The Trouble With Turkeys
Christmas Crazy
Cupid's Curse
Big Bunny Bump-off
Beach Blanket Barbie
Maui Madness
Derby Divas
Haunted Hamlet
Halloween Hijinks Anniversary Edition –September 2014
Turkeys, Tuxes, and Tabbies– October 2014
Christmas Cozy – November 2014
Alaskan Alliance – December 2014

Road to Christmas Romance:
Road to Christmas Past

Chapter 1

Friday, November 21

"It's starting to snow," Tj Jensen said to her best friends, Jenna Elston, Kyle Donovan, and Nikki Weston, as she joined them at their regular table at Murphy's Bar. It was the start of the Thanksgiving break, giving Tj an entire week off from her job as a high-school coach and teacher.

"I heard a major storm might blow in by the end of next week," Kyle added as he poured Tj a beer from the pitcher. "They're predicting as much as four feet of fresh powder."

"That's a lot for this time of year," Jenna said. "Maybe Bonnie's new boyfriend will decide to cancel his visit and I won't have to spend the Thanksgiving holiday visiting my husband in jail."

"I'm sure it won't be that bad." Tj laughed as she waved at one of the waitresses, who was decorating the most pathetic Christmas tree she had ever seen. It was hard to believe it was only a little over a month until Santa would make his magical ride. Tj loved Christmas, but it represented an increase in her workload. She might have three weeks off from her job as a coach and physical education teacher at Serenity High School, but there was always tons of decorating, shopping, wrapping, and baking to do, in addition to the extra work she usually took on at the resort.

"Don't be too sure about that." Jenna's tone portrayed an element of doom. "When Dennis finds out his mother is engaged to a man she's only known for two months, he's going to hit the roof."

"I can't believe you haven't told him about it by now," Kyle commented as he picked at one of the buffalo wings the group was sharing.

"I keep hoping Bonnie will come to her senses and call the whole thing off," Jenna admitted. "I know Dennis seems like a mild-mannered kind of guy, but when it comes to his mother . . ."

"I have a feeling I'm coming into this conversation in the middle of the movie," Nikki said with a laugh.

While Jenna was Tj's best lifelong friend and Kyle was her best new friend, Nikki was her best work friend, a teacher at Serenity High School who had been dating the football coach for the past year. Prior to her relationship with Carl, Nikki had hung out with Tj and Jenna quite a bit, but after she became romantically involved with a man who had his own friends and interests, the amount of time she spent with Tj had decreased dramatically. Things had changed, though, when Carl had been offered a job coaching football at a large college in Los Angles. While Nikki and Carl cared about each other, neither was willing to go so far as to make a permanent commitment, and the job, they both agreed, was too good to pass up. After quite a bit of angst and considerable conversation, the two had decided to break up. Carl's last day at Serenity High School had been two weeks earlier, and Nikki had taken his leaving harder than she imagined she would. This was the first time she had felt good enough to go out for a drink with the gang.

"Bonnie," Jenna said, referring to her mother-in-law, "met a man named Bob King back in August, and he invited her to attend a retreat geared toward restaurant owners and chefs in September. I guess while they were there they developed a romantic relationship of an unspecified nature. Bob lives in Los Angeles, so once the retreat was over they went their separate ways but kept in touch. A few weeks ago Bonnie flew to Los Angeles to visit him, and when she came home she announced to me that she was engaged."

"Wow," Nikki said. "And you haven't told Dennis?"

"Not yet. Dennis's parents were high-school sweethearts. Bonnie had never dated anyone other than Dennis's father until this Bob King. I realize Dennis's father has been dead for quite some time, and Bonnie might want to move on with her life, but I'm fairly certain Dennis won't see it that way. I've been looking for the right time to tell him, but so far that time really hasn't presented itself."

"I've made all the arrangements for Mr. King to stay in one of the empty cabins," Tj assured her. "I figure that way we can keep an eye on him. If Dennis does go ballistic, maybe his being at the resort will help us control the situation."

"I really want to thank you for doing this. I know the resort is closed for the fall holiday and most of your staff is away on vacation. If I wasn't so nervous about things, I'd just have him check into a hotel in town."

"It's not a problem," Tj assured her. "The staff might be off for the holiday, but there will be plenty of family on site to see to things. What time should we expect Mr. King?"

"Bonnie is picking him up from the airport in Reno on Wednesday morning. She plans to bring him by the house to meet Dennis. I imagine he'll stay for dinner, so I guess Bonnie will bring him by after that, if Dennis hasn't killed him by then. Of course, he might prefer to drop off his luggage and then come out to the house. I can have Bonnie text you and let you know when you should expect him."

"And Thanksgiving?" Tj asked.

"I don't know. I haven't thought that far ahead. At this point I'm just trying to get past Wednesday with no bloodshed."

"Why don't you and your family come out to the resort for Thanksgiving dinner and I can help you prevent your firefighter hubby from ax murdering his mom's new boyfriend?" Tj suggested. "Besides, maybe you can prevent me from using Dennis's ax on Captain Jordan Tanner; I just received confirmation that he'll arrive on Wednesday as well."

Jenna squeezed Tj's hand. "I'm sorry. Here I am, going on and on about my Thanksgiving mess, and you're dealing with so much more."

Tj sighed. "I have to admit I've been a bundle of nerves since the moment I got the letter from Tanner's attorney last summer, hoping for the best but mentally preparing for the worst."

"Again," Nikki commented, "I have no idea what you're talking about. Maybe it's not such a bad thing that Carl was offered that job in LA. I've really been out of the loop lately."

Tj looked at Jenna and Kyle. Both shrugged. She seemed to come to a decision. "What I'm going to tell you is a secret. A *big* secret. No one knows about this except my dad and grandpa, Jenna, Kyle, and Hunter. You have to swear not to mention it to anyone."

"Yeah, okay." Nikki paled. "What's wrong?"

"I got a certified letter from an attorney last summer, informing me that his client, a man named Jordan Tanner, had been informed by one of my mom's old friends that he might be the biological father of my sister Gracie."

"He finds out he's a father last summer and isn't visiting until now?"

"Jordan Tanner is a captain in the Navy and has been at sea since May of last year. This is the first opportunity he's had to follow up on the letter. He admitted that he had a one-night stand with a woman meeting my mom's description prior to shipping out for a six-month tour seven years ago, but he swears he had no communication with the woman after that night."

"So why does he believe he's Gracie's father?" Nikki wondered. "Your mom's friend could have been wrong or even lying."

"I did a background check on the man," Kyle informed her. "There were photos. Captain Tanner has dark hair, dark eyes, and a dark complexion. He looks a lot like Gracie, whereas Tj, Ashley, Tj's mom, and the girls' father, all have very different coloring."

"To be honest, I've always suspected Ashley and Gracie might not be full sisters," Tj admitted. "My mother looked a lot like me. She was petite, with dark auburn curly hair, blue eyes, and fair skin. The girls' father, Jonathan Howard, was tall and thin, with light reddish-blond hair and green eyes. As you know, Ashley has straight red hair, green eyes, fair skin, and a nose covered with freckles. Gracie, on the other hand, has thick curly brown hair, brown eyes, and darker skin than anyone in either the Jensen or Howard families."

"I see your point. After your mom died in that car accident and you brought the girls to live with you, I remember wondering if they had different fathers. It didn't seem all that important, so I didn't ask about it. You were all going through so much with the adjustment. After I got to know the girls they seemed so much like sisters that I never gave it a second thought. Does this man want custody?" Nikki asked.

"The attorney says no. He insists Captain Tanner wants nothing more than to meet Gracie. He's arranged to spend a month at Maggie's Hideaway over the holidays, while he's on leave."

"Wow. No wonder you've been so distracted lately. I just assumed your funk was due to the fact that Dylan left."

"No. I'm over Dylan," Tj said. "At first I was pretty bummed, but I've had time to gain some perspective and I realize we never really had a future. I've spoken to him a few times since the move and he seems happy. He likes his new job and his sister is beginning to relax. It means a lot to him that he's able to be an everyday part of his nephew's life. I think in the long run he made the right decision."

"So you and Hunter . . . ?" Nikki asked.

Hunter Hanson had been Tj's high-school boyfriend and the rock she had been leaning on since she'd received the letter that had tossed her world off its axis.

"Friends," Tj answered.

"Yeah right," Jenna snorted.

Tj gave Jenna the *look*, which warned her that Hunter, and her relationship with him, was a subject she didn't care to discuss.

"So about Thanksgiving . . ." Tj changed the subject to a safer topic. Her feelings for Hunter were complicated and not at all something she was willing or able to deal with at that moment in time.

"I think it's a wonderful idea for us to all have Thanksgiving together," Jenna said. "We can help each other get through the day."

Tj turned to Nikki. "You're invited as well."

"Thanks, I'd like that."

"Would you, your mom, and the girls like to come as well?" Tj asked Kyle.

"Yeah, that would be nice. Kiara will be home, so I'm sure she'd love to visit with you."

Kiara Boswell and her sister Annabeth had moved in with Kyle's mother, who had recently moved to Serenity to be near her only son, after their father was arrested for kidnapping both Kiara and Tj the previous summer.

"I'd love to see Kiara." Tj smiled. "It's been months. Will she be here for the entire holiday season?"

"She has to go back to school for finals after Thanksgiving, but she'll be home in time for the play and won't need to go back to school until after New Year's."

Kyle had arranged for Kiara to attend community college in preparation for transferring to a four-year university the following year. Both Kiara and Annabeth had been raised without a formal education but both were thriving under Kyle and his mother's care.

"Speaking of the play, are you still planning to hold rehearsals next week?" Tj asked.

Ashley and Gracie, as well as Jenna's daughters, Kristi and Kari, were cast members in *The Best Christmas Pageant Ever*, which was being produced by both Kyle and Jenna.

"On Monday and Tuesday," Kyle answered. "Then we'll take the rest of the week off and resume our rehearsals the week after Thanksgiving."

"I'm glad you aren't practicing on Wednesday. I suddenly realized I have a ton to do and only a short time to get it done."

"I'll help you with the food," Jenna offered. "I know I cook for a living, but I really enjoy making Thanksgiving dinner. How many turkeys do you think we'll need?" Jenna owned the Antiquery, a coffee shop and antique store, with her mom Helen and mother-in-law Bonnie.

Tj thought about it. "I know Dad invited Rosalie"—she referred to her father's girlfriend, town veterinarian Rosalie Taylor—"so that's two. Grandpa invited Doc and Bookman, which brings us to five. If you add in Ashley, Gracie, Captain Tanner, and me, that makes nine. There are four of you plus your mom, Bonnie, and Bonnie's new guy, so that brings us to sixteen. Add Nikki, Kyle, his mom, Kiara, and Annabeth and we have twenty-one."

"Anyone else?" Jenna asked.

"Actually, I thought about asking Hunter and Jake, since I heard Chelsea is going back east this year to visit their parents. If they want to come over, that will be two more. I think that's it. At least for now," Tj confirmed.

"What about Bren?" Kyle asked about Jenna's sister.

"I'm not sure what she's planning to do," Jenna answered. "She mentioned something about making dinner for Pastor Dan and Hannah at one point."

Tj knew that Jenna's younger sister babysat part-time for the four-year-old daughter of the pastor of the Serenity Community Church. Dan's wife had died when Hannah was just a baby and the members of the close-knit congregation all pitched in to help out.

"Invite them to come to our dinner if you want," Tj suggested. "We can use the kitchen in the Grill and the big activities room for the dinner if we need to since the resort is closed."

"Okay, I'll ask her. If they want to come, that will bring us to twenty-six. I can't believe how fast the holiday season has snuck up on us. It's going to be a busy month with the play, in addition to all of the usual holiday events we attend every year."

"I saw they brought the tree in for the tree lighting next Friday," Nikki informed the group. "It seems like the town could just use one of the big trees in the park rather than cutting one and having it hauled into town every year."

"They like to set it up right next to the gazebo, but I see your point about using a tree that's already growing in the park," Tj said. "There are a few really nice ones near the children's play area that would work well, and we could even buy extra lights and decorate the really tall white fir near the benches that overlook the lake. Of course, neither of those locations would provide as nice a platform for the choir to perform during the lighting ceremony."

Tj turned to Kyle. "Which reminds me: did you ever manage to get any volunteers from the choir for the tree lighting?" Tj was the official choir director for Serenity High School, but Kyle, being much more musically inclined, had taken over as unofficial volunteer choir director.

"I have eight confirmed and three maybes," Kyle informed her. "We've been practicing for the past few weeks, so I feel confident we'll put on a show you can be proud of. Two of the freshman girls we recruited this year have volunteered to do solos. They both have fantastic voices, which makes me think we have a real chance to at least place in this year's show choir competition. I got a few of the returning students to step up and take the lead for the tree lighting. I think you're going to be pleasantly surprised by the group."

"Excellent." Tj sighed in relief. "And thanks for taking the lead on this. With everything that's been going on, I haven't had the focus to devote to the choir the way I should."

Kyle shrugged. "You know I'm happy to do it. It's not like I have a lot going on otherwise."

"Of course you have a lot going on," Tj countered. "You're newly elected to the town council, which I might add was left in a bit of a mess after Mayor Wallaby resigned. Any luck finding someone new?"

"Not yet, but we're working on it. In fact, now that the position is open, we're looking at the entire process. Wallaby was hired to fill the job a lot of years ago. There are several members of the committee who want a whole new system. I'm too new to both the town and the council to have much of a perspective, but at least Bookman decided not to resign. We plan to go ahead with some sort of recruitment after the first of the year; in the meantime, the council is handling the town business with Harriet's help." Harriet Kramer was the mayor's secretary.

"It seems like Harriet was happy to see Wallaby go," Nikki provided. "I ran into her at the market and she made a comment that led me to believe there was more going on behind the scenes than anyone was willing to admit."

Tj laughed. "While I agree that the man's absence has made her life easier, I think it has also left a hole in the local gossip network. The mayor may have had multiple problems, but he was a colorful man who always provided interesting tidbits for Harriet to 'leak' to the gals at the Antiquery."

"It *has* been quiet of late," Jenna admitted. "Which, in the long run, affects business. Nothing gets people to come in for coffee and dessert like a good bit of gossip provided by Mom and Bonnie."

Tj looked out the window. "It looks like the storm is getting worse. We should all head home while we can. You still up for some Christmas shopping tomorrow?" she asked Jenna.

"Maybe. I have the day off from the Antiquery, so it would be a good day to go, but I don't really want to make the drive down the mountain if the roads are bad. I guess we could postpone to next weekend if we have to."

"The stores will be packed Thanksgiving weekend. Maybe the following weekend, although I hate to leave it so late. You remember what happened last year."

The previous Christmas had been Ashley and Gracie's first without their mother. Tj had done everything in her power to make it special, but she'd waited too long to start her shopping and hadn't been able to find the doll Gracie swore her mother had promised Santa would bring her before she died. Tj had almost killed herself trying to track it down, driving hundreds of miles to every toy store in the state before Kyle had managed to pull some strings to get the doll directly from the manufacturer. Tj was pretty sure that Miss Daisy, as Gracie called her, was the most expensive doll on the face of the earth. It was a good thing her good friend Zachary Collins had left his very generous grandson his fortune when he died. Kyle seemed to always put the money to good use, while Tj knew there were others who wouldn't.

"I need to buy a couple hundred toys for the toy drive at the church," Kyle said. "I'm putting in a huge order, so if there's anything specific you need, I can probably get it for you at the same time."

"Actually, that would be very helpful," Tj replied. "I'll talk to the girls this weekend to see if I can get a list. When are you placing the order?"

"Monday or Tuesday."

"Can I get in on this?" Jenna asked.

"Just give me a list and Santa Kyle will see what he can do."

"Can I get you anything else?" The waitress, who had been tying red ribbons on the tree she was decorating, asked, noticing their empty pitcher.

TJ shook her head. "No thanks. I think we're about done."

"I'll get your check."

"Are you going to give out the toys again?" Jenna asked as the waitress walked away.

Last year Kyle had dressed as Santa, borrowed a sleigh with four horses from Maggie's Hideaway, and then personally delivered gifts to all the children on the list Pastor Dan had given him.

"Absolutely. I can't remember the last time I had that much fun. Annabeth wants to be an elf this year. I was hoping you could help with a costume," Kyle said to Jenna, who not only was a great cook but a fabulous seamstress who usually made the costumes for the plays she and Kyle enjoyed putting on for the community.

"I'd be happy to make an elf costume for Annabeth. Bring her by so I can discuss her preferences and get some measurements."

"Thanks. I really appreciate your help. My mom volunteered to do it, but she really doesn't have a clue what type of costume a preteen might prefer."

"She still trying to dress her in outfits that might be better suited for a convent?" Jenna laughed.

"She tries, and Annabeth is too polite to refuse to wear the clothes Mom buys her. I took Annabeth shopping myself when school started and we've been weeding out Mom's old-fashioned dresses for something more decade appropriate."

"Speaking of age appropriate," Tj interrupted, "did you see that young guy Frannie's been parading around town?"

"It is a little odd that after all these years she'd choose him as her first serious boyfriend," Jenna agreed. "What is he, like thirty-five?"

"Seems about right," Tj said.

Frannie Edison was the never married—and, as far as anyone knew, never dated—town librarian. She was in her midfifties and the man she had been seen around town with looked to be at least two decades younger.

"We don't actually know that he's her boyfriend," Nikki pointed out. "They've been spending a lot of time together, but I have yet to witness a physical exchange more intimate than hand-holding. Maybe he's a nephew or the son of an old friend."

"Maybe I'll invite them to the Thanksgiving dinner as well," Tj decided. "I'd like to get a chance to chat with the guy to make sure his intentions toward our Frannie are honorable, if he indeed is boyfriendish in nature."

"Intentions?" Kyle asked. "You aren't her mother."

"I know, but I am her friend and I don't want to see her get hurt. She seems so vulnerable and untried in the ways of love. It would be easy for some guy to take advantage of her naïve and kind heart."

"I'm not sure Frannie is as helpless as you make her out to be, but it would be nice to invite her to dinner." Jenna took out her notepad and added Frannie and friend to her list. "That gives us twenty-eight. I think we're going to need at least two birds. Big ones."

"I'd get three for this beast of a feast," Tj said.

Chapter 2

Monday, November 24

"Look at all the lights," Gracie screeched with delight as Tj drove her sisters to play practice. It looked as though the community volunteers had been out in force over the weekend; every window on Main Street was framed with white lights and every lamppost sported a pine wreath tied up with a huge red ribbon. The fresh coat of snow that had fallen over the past few days gave the mountain hamlet the feel of an authentic Christmas village.

"Can we go look at the windows?" Gracie asked as Tj began searching for a parking spot.

"Maybe after Thanksgiving," Tj said. "We have rehearsal tonight and tomorrow night and then a very busy couple of days making a huge feast for everyone we've invited for dinner on Thanksgiving."

"Kristi wants to come over early to watch the parade with us," Ashley announced.

"I'll have to talk to Aunt Jenna about it, but I imagine she'll come early as well since she's making most of the food."

"How come Aunt Jenna is making the food if it's at our house?" Gracie asked.

"'Cause Tj can't cook," Ashley explained.

"I can too cook," Tj defended herself.

"Really? You burned the toast we had for breakfast and the eggs were so runny that Grandpa had to make us pancakes."

"Eggs are tricky," Tj commented.

Ashley rolled her eyes in the condescending way only she could.

"Are we going to be able to go to the tree lighting again like we did last year?" Gracie thankfully changed the subject.

Tj slowed as a group of shoppers crossed the street. With all the fresh snow, everyone was bundled up in heavy coats, knit hats, and scarves, making it almost impossible to definitively identify the passersby, but Tj was fairly certain the pedestrians were students who had skipped school today due to the sudden onset of a flu that had, interestingly enough, only affected their little crowd.

"Of course. We go every year," Tj said after making a mental note to speak to the students in question. There wasn't a single teen among them who could afford to miss class if they hoped to graduate at the end of the school year.

"Since it snowed, can we take the sleigh to the tree lighting?" Ashley asked.

"If Papa agrees," Tj answered.

"Can Kristi and Kari come with us?" Ashley added.

"I'm not sure we'll have enough room," Tj said. "We're having a visitor at the resort this year." She'd decided to take this opportunity to broach the subject she'd been steadfastly avoiding.

"A kid?" Gracie wondered.

"No, an adult. He's in the Navy and his name is Captain Tanner. He's going to be staying in one of the cabins until after Christmas, so I thought it would be nice to invite him to come along with us to the tree lighting. If he does want to come, we won't have room for Kristi and Kari unless we bring a second sleigh."

"Does Captain Tanner have kids?" Gracie asked.

"No," Tj choked. "It will be just him staying at the resort."

"He doesn't like kids?"

"I'm sure he likes kids, Gracie, it's just that as an officer in the Navy, he's away at sea a large portion of the time," Tj explained.

"Why can't he take his kids with him?" she asked.

"Don't be stupid," Ashley spat. "People in the Navy live on boats. It's their job to be far out in the ocean. They can't bring their kids."

"I'm not stupid," Gracie argued.

"Let's not fight, and Ashley, don't call your sister stupid," Tj reprimanded. She really didn't want to talk any more about Jordan Tanner, so she decided to change the subject. "As long as we're on the subject of Christmas, what are you both planning to ask Santa for?"

Tj slowed as they drove by the park, which was decorated with lights in the evergreen trees, as well as others outlining the gazebo. Once they lit the hundred-foot town Christmas tree on Friday, it was going to be spectacular.

"There is no—"

"Ashley . . ." Tj warned.

Ashley stopped speaking. Tj had told her numerous times not to ruin her sister's fun by pointing out that the man in the jolly red suit was a mythological being and not a real, flesh-and-blood man.

"No what?" Gracie asked.

"No reason why we can't ask for more than one gift." Ashley cleverly used Tj's diversion to her advantage. "I've been really good this year and I really want a cell phone *and* a new computer."

"We talked about the phone thing," Tj reminded her. "Not until middle school."

"All my friends have phones," Ashley said.

"No," Tj corrected, "they don't."

"I want a doll," Gracie joined in.

"You got a doll last year," Tj reminded her.

"I'm thinking about expanding my family."

Tj smiled. "Expanding your family?"

"That's what Kari told me Jenna and Dennis want to do, but the stork is having problems. I told them that they should look on the Internet for a baby. My teacher says you can get anything on Amazon."

Tj tried not to laugh at Gracie's serious tone of voice. She was really thinking through this expanding-her-family idea.

"I don't think you can get a baby on Amazon, but your teacher isn't all that far off otherwise. What kind of a doll would you like to ask Santa for?"

Gracie considered for a moment. "I'm not sure. Maybe one with curly brown hair like mine. The doll I got last year had long blond hair, and even though she's pretty, she doesn't look like she would be my baby. She looks like she would be Kari's baby, or maybe Kristi's, since Kristi and Kari both have long blond hair like Aunt Jenna."

"So about the computer . . ." Ashley brought the conversation back around to her true desire.

"Computers are expensive," Tj pointed out.

"Which is why I'm asking Santa and not you." Ashley grinned. "Santa makes things in his workshop, so he doesn't have to worry about how much stuff costs."

"That's true," Gracie backed up her sister.

Tj sighed. It wasn't pretty when you were outsmarted by an eight-year-old.

"I'm not sure Santa brings computers," Tj tried.

"Three kids in my class got computers from Santa last year," Ashley insisted.

Tj didn't want to have this conversation in front of Gracie. Ashley could be sweet, but she could also be manipulative. If push came to shove, she might ruin Gracie's belief in Santa if she thought it would help her get what she wanted. In many ways she was a lot like their mother. Tj just hoped she'd come into Ashley's life early enough to turn things around.

"Okay," Tj gave in. "I guess it wouldn't hurt to *ask* Santa for a computer, but you should have a backup as well, in case Santa is out of computers by the time he gets to Paradise Lake."

"I won't need a backup," Ashley assured her. "Everyone knows Santa is branching off into electronics. I hear he has a whole crew of elves devoted to nothing but building and developing cool equipment. Not only does he bring things like cell phones and computers but he brings iPods and televisions too. Next year I'm going to ask for a flat screen, but for now a computer is fine."

Tj groaned quietly as she calculated the cost of a new computer. Although, the more she thought about it, getting Ashley her own computer might not be such a bad idea. Her sister was smart. Really smart. She had a ton of potential and knew more about technology than Tj ever would. And she did have the coin collection her friend Zachary had left her when he died. Tj had been trying to avoid cashing in any of the coins until it was time to pay for the girls' college education, but a computer was an educational gift. So maybe . . .

"And I'll need a graphics card and extra memory too," Ashley added. "And a decent processor; not one of those ancient ones that takes forever to load. Oh, and a camera, so I can Skype. I'll write it all down for you."

Tj cleared her throat.

"For you to give to Santa," Ashley added.

"Do you think Santa has a doll with a red dress and brown eyes?" Gracie added.

Lord, I hope so.

"It's really disturbing what a believable Gladys Ashley makes," Tj whispered to Jenna as the kids rehearsed their lines. The character of Gladys Herdman was a feisty, imaginative preteen who stuck up for herself and liked to fight. Talk about typecasting.

Jenna laughed as she watched the rehearsal from the back of the room. Kyle had asked her to sit in the rear for a scene so they could get an idea of how well the kids could be heard from all parts of the makeshift theater.

"I have to admit I was glad when Annabeth got the part of Imogene Herdman and Kristi got Alice Wendleken," Jenna replied. "Kristi really wanted to be Imogene, but Kristi has a very vivid imagination, and I was afraid she'd channel the personality of the part she was going to portray. Alice is an annoying character, but she's still better than having a little rebel under my roof for eight weeks."

"How did you get Eric Clayton to play Ralph Herdman?" Tj asked. Eric *was* for all intents and purposes Ralph, a streetwise adolescent who took care of himself much of the time while his mom had been working two jobs to support her family after her husband left her.

"Kyle worked out a deal with him. I didn't want to know the details so I didn't ask, but I'm pretty sure he promised to help him out with Christmas gifts for his younger siblings."

"I'm sure the Clayton kids are on Dan's list anyway," Tj said.

"True, but I got the feeling Eric wanted something specific. Something expensive."

Tj rolled her eyes. "What is it with kids and expensive gifts? Ashley has all but blackmailed me into getting her a computer for Christmas."

"Blackmailed?"

"She's going to ask *Santa* for it. I have a feeling if I want her to keep the Santa secret for Gracie's sake, Santa will need to come through."

Jenna grinned. "The girl is crafty. What does Gracie want?"

"A doll that looks like her. One with a red dress." Tj sighed. "I don't know what I'll do if I lose her."

"You won't lose her."

"We don't know that," Tj argued. "Jordan Tanner is her biological father. I'm sure that if he sued for custody he'd get it. I'm only her sister. Her half sister."

"First of all, you don't know for certain that Mr. Tanner is Gracie's father, and even if he is, the man is in the Navy. What would he do with a child?"

"Once he gets a look at that angelic little face, he's going to want her. I mean, really, who could resist?"

Jenna turned and looked directly at Tj. "Gracie *is* adorable, but you have to try to stay positive through this process. If you feel fear, the girls will sense it and be fearful as well. Are you going to tell them what's really going on?"

Tj tucked her feet up under her body. One advantage to being petite was that she could curl up in small places. She nervously nibbled on one of her thumbnails as she responded. "I haven't discussed it with Captain Tanner, but I'm hoping he'll see the wisdom in leaving well enough alone. If he wants to have some sort of relationship with Gracie, I hope he'll tell the girls he's some sort of honorary uncle or something. My stomach gets all knotted up every time I consider the possible outcomes of this visit."

Jenna put her arm around Tj's shoulder and gave it a squeeze. "I know you're scared and I really do understand. I don't know what I'd do if I was in your situation. I just want to remind you that I'm here for you, as are Kyle, Nikki, and Hunter."

"Thanks; I appreciate that."

"I need to get back for this next scene. Will you be okay?" Jenna asked.

"I'll be fine. Can I help?"

Jenna hesitated. "Actually, if you don't mind, Eric really needs to work on his lines. Maybe you could run through the next scene with him a few times while Kyle and I get the baby angels ready to go on."

"Yeah, okay, I can do that. Gracie and Kari really are adorable as baby angels," Tj commented as she and Jenna made their way to the stage of the community center.

"I wish we could do a play with all baby angels." Jenna sighed. "They're all so sweet and excited just to be included in the event. The older kids tend to be a bit harder to handle. I can't believe how many diva attitudes we've had to deal with, and our oldest actor is only fifteen."

"Maybe the older kids are more demanding, but they don't have to be watched quite as closely as the younger ones. Since I've been sitting here, I've seen two baby angels take off running up the aisle."

"You have a point," Jenna admitted. "I wanted to require that all the kids be at least in first grade, but then Bren asked me to make an exception for Hannah. I almost said no, but she insisted that Hannah really wanted to do it and would be fine following directions. She really has been an angel. She's much better behaved than most kids her age."

"I guess if your dad is a preacher you have to be on your best behavior most of the time, and Bren has been really good with her."

Jenna lowered her voice and leaned in close. "I don't know this for a fact, so please don't say anything, but I think there might be something going on between Bren and Pastor Dan."

"Really? Something romantic?"

"His wife has been gone for several years now, and Bren has started spending a lot of time over at his house. At first she was just helping out with Hannah, but lately . . ."

Tj thought about it. She supposed that pastors shared a desire for romance, intimacy, and family, just like the rest of the population. Bren was quite a bit younger than Dan, but she was sweet and very mature, in spite of the fact that she was a drummer in an all-girl metal band.

"You know," Tj whispered, "I think you might be right. I noticed that she dyed her purple strip brown to match the rest of her hair, and she's removed both her tongue and her eyebrow rings. It seems like she's cleaned up the way she dresses as well. Having said that, I have to say I've never pictured her as a preacher's wife. She was always such a rebel."

"She's still pretty independent," Jenna said. "And she's a long way away from being anyone's wife, but I can see that she's good for Dan and he's good for her. He seems less formal and a lot more relaxed and she seems to be more serious and responsible."

"What does your mom think?" Tj wondered.

"Mom hasn't said anything, so I'm assuming she hasn't yet made the connection between Bren's job as a nanny and her new adult approach to life. I don't think my mom will have a problem with a relationship between Bren and Dan, if it comes to that, but sometimes Mom can be unpredictable. I figure I'll keep my suspicions to myself for now and see how things work out."

"It went well tonight," Jenna commented to Kyle after he'd called an end to rehearsal and the parents had taken their little darlings home.

"It does seem like things are starting to come together," Kyle agreed. "Frannie came by earlier and worked with some of the kids who have the most lines. I think the extra rehearsal really helped."

"That was nice of her," Jenna said.

Kyle looked at Tj. "She mentioned she was coming to Thanksgiving at the resort and planned to bring her friend Arnie, but she told me that she was going to ask you if it would be okay to invite Hazel as well. I told her I was sure it would be fine and I'd bring it up to you tonight."

Hazel Whipple was the town's seventy-three-year-old postmistress. "It's fine. I should have thought of inviting her myself. I also invited my new restaurant manager, Kallie Wilson. I found out she wasn't going home as planned. So I guess we need to add two more to the list," Tj informed Jenna.

"Actually, make it four more. Dennis invited Josh and Captain Brown as well. The two of them volunteered to be on call since neither of them has any family in town, but they figured if they brought the engine out to the resort they could respond from there if they got a call. With all this snow, it seems unlikely there'll be a fire, but you never know when someone will burn the house down trying to cook a turkey."

Josh Green was Dennis's engine mate and best friend and Captain Brown was the head of the Serenity fire department. Dennis had mentioned that the captain usually spent holidays alone since his parents passed and his sister had been killed in an accident several years back.

"So what is that? Thirty-two?" Tj asked.

Jenna quickly added up the names on her list. "Looks like. We'll need at least four birds if we hope to have leftovers for sandwiches. I have plenty of potatoes and ingredients for stuffing, gravy, and a couple of veggie side dishes."

"My mom said she'd bring a couple of salads," Kyle offered, "and Frannie said she and Hazel would each bring a dessert."

"Nikki is bringing an appetizer she's been dying to try out and Kallie will want to provide something," Tj added. "She's a really good cook, so she can probably handle anything you need. If you want to give me a list of who you want to bring what, I can call everyone."

"It'll be easier if I just do it. Can you provide the beer, wine, coffee, and soft drinks?" Jenna asked Tj.

"Done. I'll make a rum punch as well. I know Logan stocked the bar before he left for vacation," Tj said, referring to the Maggie's Hideaway bartender. "I'm sure he won't mind if I pillage his supplies."

"Perfect. We're closing the Antiquery from noon Wednesday until Friday, so I'll come over on Wednesday and help you set everything up. There are quite a few things I can do the day before, like bake the rolls, make the pies, and chop the veggies."

"What about Bonnie and her new guy?" Tj asked. "Aren't you supposed to spend Wednesday making sure your hubby doesn't kill his new daddy?"

"Oh, yeah." Jenna sighed. "I guess I was blocking that out."

"I'll help you on Thursday," Tj promised. "We can get everything ready in plenty of time."

"I can come over early on Thanksgiving as well," Kyle offered. "Just let me know if you need me to bring anything other than the salads my mom has already promised."

"You may need to restrain Jenna and me, depending on how our initial impressions of our out-of-town guests go, so handcuffs and some strong rope might be a good idea."

Kyle laughed. "I really hope it doesn't come to that."

"I guess it depends on whether this Navy man has designs on my Gracie."

"I keep telling you it most likely will be fine," Jenna reminded Tj.

"And you might really like Bonnie's new guy," Tj pointed out.

"Honestly, I hope I do. And I hope Dennis likes him even more. Bonnie has always had a level head on her shoulders, so maybe she really did meet the perfect guy."

"By the way . . ." Tj turned to Kyle and lowered her voice. The girls were playing on the stage, out of earshot. "Ashley wants a computer for Christmas and Gracie wants a doll with curly brown hair, brown eyes, and a red dress."

Kyle smiled. "I have the perfect computer in mind for Ashley. She'll love it. And it comes in colors too. I seem to remember her having a fondness for purple."

"Yeah, she does like purple. But I can't spend a fortune on Christmas gifts, so look for a deal."

"Don't worry. I have connections. I can get an awesome computer for less than a cheap one in a retail store."

"And the doll?"

Kyle grinned. "Just leave it up to Santa Kyle."

Chapter 3

Wednesday, November 26

"He's late." Tj squeezed Hunter's hand as they waited for Jordan Tanner to make an appearance at Hunter's office. They had talked about it and decided it might be a good idea to talk to the man privately before they took him out to the resort and introduced him to the family.

"He's only fifteen minutes late," Hunter said. "His plane could have been delayed, and with the snow we've had the past few days, the roads are probably icy. He'll be here."

Tj actually hoped he didn't show. Ever. But she didn't say as much. She'd gone through every possible scenario in her head dozens of times, and any way you sliced it, the man posed a threat to all she held dear. Yes, he was in the armed services, and that was a noble calling. And yes, it was easy to see how a night of passion could lead to the unknown birth of a child. And everyone who knew of Jordan Tanner's existence had assured her on multiple occasions that the man most likely had only the purest of intentions. But Tj didn't want Gracie to have a biological father who might come to love her and want to spend time with her. As selfish as it might be, she didn't want to share her baby sister with anyone. Did that make her a bad person? Maybe it did, but all Tj knew was that the mere thought of someone taking her place in

Gracie's life filled her with a terror she didn't have any idea how to deal with.

"And everything seemed okay when you spoke to him on the phone yesterday?" Tj asked for the tenth time.

"Everything seemed fine," Hunter assured her. "He was very polite and seemed appreciative that we were going out of our way to accommodate his schedule. He reiterated that he would be shipping out after the first of the year, and he didn't say anything that led me to believe his intentions were anything other than what he's already stated. He simply wants to meet his daughter and satisfy himself that she's in a good place. It sounded like he'd already checked you out and was happy about what he'd learned."

"He checked me out?" Tj tried for just the right amount of outrage.

"You had Kyle check him out," Hunter pointed out.

"I know." Tj got up and began pacing back and forth across the office. "I can't remember the last time I was this nervous. What if he turns out to be a creep? What if he really is after custody of Gracie? Or money? He probably wants money."

"It is very unlikely that the man wants money. The problem is that you've had months to imagine every possible outcome to this meeting and you've let your imagination run amok," Hunter said. "What's going to happen is going to happen. We'll deal with whatever presents itself. You need to relax. It seems like you're needlessly making yourself nuts."

"Needlessly? This man has the power to take Gracie from me. What do you know? You don't have any kids."

Hunter got up and walked around the desk, then put his arms around Tj and pulled her tight against his chest. Tj initially tried to fight him but then gave way to the comfort Hunter's arms had always provided. She listened to his heartbeat count away the seconds as they waited for destiny to arrive. After only a few minutes there was a knock on the door.

"Ready?" Hunter smiled at her.

"As ready as I'll ever be."

Tj had seen photos of Captain Tanner, enough photos to determine that based on physical similarities, he was most likely Gracie's biological father. She thought she was prepared to meet the man who so closely resembled the sister she loved. She'd certainly pictured this moment dozens of times. But in spite of her daydreams, she was *not* prepared for the commanding presence of the tall, muscular naval officer who had the darkest brown eyes she had ever seen.

"Captain Tanner," Hunter greeted as he opened the door.

"Dr. Hanson," the man returned.

"Please call me Hunter."

The man turned to Tj after shaking Hunter's hand. "Ms. Jensen." He held out his hand to Tj and smiled as he waited for her to reply.

"Captain," Tj croaked out.

"Call me Jordan." He smiled again. "Both of you." Then he focused all of his attention on Tj. "I've been looking forward to meeting you. I've heard such wonderful things about you."

Tj felt her heart pound in her chest as she realized that the dimple on the side of his mouth had the same effect on her heart as Gracie's dimple when she grinned. Tj tried to rein in her emotions. If she wasn't careful, she was going to agree to anything the smooth-talking Navy man asked for, which was something she most definitely did *not* want to do.

"Why don't we all take a seat," Hunter suggested as he took Tj's hand and led her to the conference table on the other end of his large office. "Have you been back in port long?" he inquired politely after everyone was seated.

"A few days. I needed to take care of a few things so that I'd be free to spend the entire month at Paradise Lake. As I indicated when we spoke on the phone, I'm hoping to get to know my daughter as well as I can before I leave on my next tour."

Tj knew she should say something at this point, but other than pleading with the man not to take her sister away from her, her mind had gone blank.

"Before we take you out to the resort to meet the family, we thought we should discuss a few things," Hunter continued.

"I think that's a good idea."

Hunter looked at Tj, who replied with a look of panic.

"First of all," Hunter began on Tj's behalf, "given the circumstances, we'd like to introduce you as a friend of the family. Gracie had a tough time after her mother died. She's finally settled into a comfortable routine in which she feels safe and secure. We don't want to see that threatened."

Tj held her breath as she waited for the man to reply. His answer, she figured, would tell her a lot about his true intentions.

"I was going to suggest something similar," Jordan agreed. He looked directly at Tj. "I'll only be here for a month. It's not my intention to disrupt all of the good things you've done for Gracie. When I got the letter informing me that I might be a father, I panicked. I'm at sea the majority of my time. Many men in my position find a way to have families, but I'm not married and have no plans to change that anytime soon. There's no way I can raise a child. I want to assure you that I was very relieved to hear that you were willing to continue on as Gracie's guardian."

Tj signed in relief. "I'm very happy to hear that."

"I realize we both have only the word of your mother's friend that I even *am* Gracie's biological father. I'm willing to take a paternity test if you'd like."

Tj looked at Hunter. They'd talked about having a formal test done when the captain arrived. He looked like Gracie, but she realized that many men had brown hair and brown eyes, though not everyone had the little girl's dimple.

"I think that for now we're fine with introducing you as a friend of the family," Tj answered. "As long as you're content in the role of a friend, I don't think testing will be necessary just yet."

"Very well."

"How about we refer to you as Uncle Jordan?" Tj suggested. "The girls have several honorary uncles in their lives, including Hunter. They understand that an honorary uncle is a special kind of friend who might not be family but is more than just a friend."

"Uncle Jordan is fine. Do you have any questions for me?"

Tj considered the broad-shouldered man as she gathered her thoughts. She could tell by the way he held himself that he was used to being in charge of everyone and everything around him, including, she imagined, his own emotions. It was hard for her to imagine the man with her mother, who had always been such a mess. Tj loved her mother in her own way, but she had always realized that she'd never been one who'd been able to take care of her own needs, let alone the needs of her children, for long periods of time.

"Did you know my mother was married when you . . . when Gracie was conceived?"

Jordan hesitated before answering. "I met your mother in a bar on the night before I was about to ship out. We were both alone and got to talking, and one thing led to another. We didn't even exchange last names. In fact, we barely spoke at all about our lives outside the bar. I'm not normally so casual in my relationships, but I was lonely and feeling bad that I didn't have anyone to miss me while I was gone. My best friend had just gotten engaged to the girl I'd been in love with since high school. I knew she loved him and would never be mine, but while I was trying to come to terms with that, I guess I just wanted companionship for one night."

"I'm sorry. That must have been hard for you," Tj sympathized.

"It was, but I've dealt with it and moved on. After I heard about Gracie, I looked back on that night and regretted that things happened the way they did."

"But back then . . .?"

"I never heard from your mother. Like I said, I didn't even know her last name, and I wasn't sure Trixie was even her real first name."

Tj laughed. "Trixie was her dog's name."

"I figured as much."

Hunter got up and poured everyone a glass of water from the pitcher he kept on the sideboard. Tj smiled at him as he set a glass in front of her. He seemed content to allow her to continue with the interview now that the ice had been broken, yet she knew that if she needed him, he'd willingly jump in.

"You must have been shocked when you got the letter from Mom's friend."

"I was more than shocked," Jordan admitted. "Initially, I figured it was a scam."

"A scam?"

"It wouldn't be the first time a woman claimed a man was the father of her child to extort money from him. After I looked into things a bit, I realized this child could actually be my daughter, so I contacted my attorney. He looked into it further, and eventually we contacted you. I realize there's a chance I might not be Gracie's father. What your mother and I had was very brief, and although I don't claim to have really known the woman, it seemed as if entering into casual relationships was something she was comfortable with."

Tj laughed. "You aren't wrong. My mom was a very special woman in her own way, but she liked variety in her love life. No offense, but you aren't at all her type. She normally went for men who were as wild as she liked to be."

"I suppose I must have caught her on a contemplative night. She seemed almost sad. It was as if she was struggling with something in her life. It was her vulnerability that drew me to her in the first place."

It was odd to think of her mom as having *real* problems. Tj'd never had much of a relationship with the woman who'd given birth to her. She'd left Tj with her dad when she was still a toddler and hadn't spent much time with her as she was growing up, although she was apt to pop in from time to time, Tj suspected, to irritate her father. When she'd gotten older, her mom began coming to her for help with one crisis after another. Tj tried to be a good daughter, but other than sending her money or bailing her out of jail, she'd never had the real relationship with her she'd longed for.

When Tj found out she'd been named Ashley and Gracie's legal guardian, she'd been both thrilled and terrified. There had always been a part of her that wanted to save the sisters she barely knew from the life she imagined they most likely led. Her mother's second husband, the girls' father, was out of the picture, so there hadn't been anyone to challenge her right to raise her sisters. Until now.

"If my mother had to have a child as a result of one of her flings then I'm glad it was with you," Tj informed the man. "Most of the men she dated really weren't the type you'd want to father your child."

"Did your mom's husband know she spent time with other men?" Jordan asked.

Tj shrugged. "I'm not certain, but I imagine he did. My mom wasn't one to be monogamous, and I'm sure all of her husbands knew that. I was only three when she left Paradise Lake, but I think she really tried with my dad. Staying in one place with one man just wasn't in her blood. She was a free spirit who lived by her own code, and the men she hooked up with usually knew the score. I actually find it comforting that she found a different type of relationship with the man responsible for my baby sister."

"Thanks, I think. I know this may sound odd, but as terrified as I was when I initially heard that I might have a child, I find the idea has grown on me. The Navy has always been my mistress, but there are times when I wonder how my life would have worked out if I'd taken a different path."

"You're younger than my mother was," Tj guessed.

"I'm thirty-eight."

"Do you have plans to retire from the Navy?"

"Not at this point."

"If you were to retire, do you foresee a future where you might want to take over as Gracie's guardian?" Tj asked.

Jordan frowned. It appeared as if he hadn't previously considered the idea. "I want what's best for my daughter, if she is indeed my daughter. At this point, it appears that living with you and your family is what's best for her. And there's the other sister to consider as well. I can assure you that I have no plans to disrupt what exists whether I'm at sea or on land."

Tj looked at Hunter. "Okay?"

He smiled back. "Okay."

Gracie loved Uncle Jordan from the moment she met him, which was odd because normally she was distrustful of strangers, especially men. Tj couldn't help but wonder if there wasn't a part of her that instinctively identified with a part of him. There wasn't really any logic in that suspicion, but on the surface it really seemed to be the only explanation.

"Is he our real uncle or our pretend uncle, like Uncle Kyle?" Gracie asked Tj later that evening as she tucked her into bed.

"He's an honorary uncle, like Uncle Kyle." Tj had decided to keep her answer simple.

"He said he lives on a big boat."

"Yes, he's in the Navy. He lives on a huge ship with hundreds of other men."

"Wow." Gracie looked impressed.

"Uncle Jordan is going to teach me to sail when he comes to visit this summer," Ashley informed her. "He said he learned to sail when he was even younger than me."

"That will be fun."

"Is Uncle Jordan going to be here for Thanksgiving *and* Christmas?" Gracie asked.

"I believe that's his plan." Tj tucked Gracie's bunny under her arm.

"We'll need to get him a sock," Gracie decided.

"A sock?" Tj asked.

"To hang on the fireplace. Me and Ashley each have one. You and Papa and Grandpa have one. Even Echo, Cuervo, Crissy, Midnight, and Snowy have one. If Uncle Jordan is going to be here, he needs one too."

"Yes," Tj realized, "I guess he does. But since he just got here, how about we see how the visit goes?"

"Okay."

"Ash, why don't you grab Snowy and head into your own room? I'll be there in a minute," Tj said as she got up from the bed and began straightening up the room. She hung up Gracie's kitty sweater and folded the clothes she'd worn for only a short time that evening.

"Okay." Ashley got up from the bed and picked up the pure white cat that had been one of the two kittens Crissy had delivered shortly after she'd come to live with them. "Don't forget the book," Ashley reminded her.

Ashley could read better than other kids three or four years older than she was, but she still enjoyed having Tj read to her as she fell asleep.

"I won't forget," Tj promised as Ashley trotted out of the room.

"Can you leave the nightlight on?" Gracie asked as Tj began turning lamps off.

"Absolutely. We have a busy day tomorrow, so I need you to go right to sleep." Tj kissed Gracie, tucking the covers around her like a cocoon. Crissy curled up on the pillow next to her and began to purr.

"Can Crissy have turkey?"

"I guess a little turkey would be okay. But just a little. We wouldn't want her to get a tummy ache."

"Okay."

Tj tucked Gracie's hair behind her ear. She loved her sister so much. In spite of Jordan's assurances and his seemingly sincere intentions, Tj couldn't help but feel a level of fear.

"Are you worried about something?" Gracie asked.

"No, I'm not worried. Why do you ask?"

"Your face is all wrinkly, like it gets when you're worried."

Tj smiled. "I guess I'm just tired. We have bunches of people coming for dinner, so I might be worried about getting everything ready in time."

"Maybe we should just have hot dogs for dinner," Gracie suggested. "Hot dogs are easy. I can make them in the microwave all by myself. If we have hot dogs for Thanksgiving, I can help you and you won't have to be worried."

"Hot dogs are a very good idea, but I already bought four turkeys. Maybe we'll have hot dogs next year. Besides, I think Aunt Jenna is going to help me, so I'm sure I'm worrying for nothing."

Gracie smiled. "I love you bunches."

"I love you bunches too."

Chapter 4

Thursday, November 27

By the time dawn arrived on Thanksgiving, the storm that had been leaving small amounts of snow for the past several days had come in with a vengeance. Tj settled Ashley and Gracie in front of the Macy's Thanksgiving Day Parade on the TV with a plate of cinnamon rolls Ben had made earlier that morning before she quickly showered and dressed for the day ahead. If today was anything like yesterday, they were in for more than one kind of storm.

"Is Uncle Jordan coming to dinner?" Gracie asked after Tj returned to the room.

"He *is* coming to dinner," Tj informed her.

"I'm glad. He's really nice."

"Yes, he is. Now finish up your breakfast and get dressed. Jenna and the girls will be here any time to help us set up."

Ashley got up from the sofa and took her plate into the kitchen, with Gracie following behind. "I'm supposed to tell you that Papa is out plowing snow and Grandpa, Doc, and Bookman are over in the restaurant getting things ready," Ashley informed her. "Grandpa said we're in for a hell of a storm and we should wear warm clothes if we go outside."

"Grandpa was right about staying warm, but I really need you to stay in the house and direct people over to the activities center when they arrive. Kristi and Kari can help you when they get here."

"Can Uncle Jordan stay here and help us?" Gracie asked.

"If he wants to," Tj answered. "I'm going to head over to the restaurant to check in with Grandpa. If Jenna gets here, send her over. I think Uncle Kyle might be coming early as well. Oh, and don't forget to feed the cats. If you need anything, call my cell."

"Okay." Ashley settled back down in front of the parade.

Tj bundled up in a heavy coat and snow boots, called to her dog, Echo, and headed out into the storm. While guest number one had so far proven to be a likeable and trustworthy sort, guest number two, Bonnie's fiancé, Bob King, was another thing entirely. Tj could tell Jenna had hated him on sight, which didn't bode well for Dennis's opinion of the man. Tj had to admit that the man had a dark aura about him. She couldn't pin it down exactly, but the charming, smooth-talking, and apparently wealthy gentleman seemed to be just a bit too slick to be real.

"Mornin', darling," Doc, aka retired coroner Stan Griffin, kissed her on the cheek as she walked into the restaurant, where all three men were mixing up batches of rum punch.

"You haven't been sampling every batch, have you?" Tj asked.

"Just the first one," Ben assured her. "Do you want a taste?"

Tj did. "This is good," she complimented. "Did you do something different?"

Rum punch was a specialty of the resort, and they had used the same recipe for years.

"Since we're giving this away and not trying to make a profit, we used some of the rum Bookman imported."

"It's really good. Maybe we should use it instead of our regular brand," Tj suggested.

Ben shook his head. "It's too expensive. We'd have to charge twenty dollars for each drink just to break even. We're just about done here and thought we'd set up the sound system in the activities room next."

"There's already a sound system set up in there," Tj reminded the man who'd built the resort two generations earlier.

"Yeah, but Bookman brought an upgrade."

Tj noticed the large speakers that were stacked near the door for the first time and rolled her eyes. Based on the size of the speakers, they were going to hear the music from the resort all the way in town. What was it with boys and their toys?

"Do you know if anyone took breakfast to our two guests?" Tj asked. Normally, the guests who stayed at the resort came into the restaurant for meals, but technically the resort was closed until the Saturday after Thanksgiving, so Tj had planned to deliver meals to the two men in their respective cabins.

"I took both of them pancakes and sausage first thing," Ben confirmed. "Captain Tanner invited me in to chat for a spell while he ate, but the other one just growled for me to go away. How long is he staying exactly?"

"Just for a few days, or until Dennis kills him, whichever comes first," Tj joked.

"I have to say I would have expected Bonnie to make a better choice," Doc commented. "The man seems to be as phony as a two-dollar bill."

"Two-dollar bills are real," Tj pointed out.

"You know what I mean. The man is just a little too smooth."

Doc had a point. Tj had felt the same thing, as had Jenna and everyone else who had met him when he arrived yesterday.

"Bonnie hasn't been in the dating game for quite some time," Bookman pointed out. "I'm sure Bob King can be quite persuasive when he wants to be. Bonnie is probably lonely since Dennis's father passed. Maybe too good to be true is exactly what she was looking for."

Ben began returning the unused rum to the locked cabinet. "Personally, I don't really trust the man. I'm not sure that Bonnie's relationship is any of our business, but I just want to go on record as saying that."

"So your other guest, this Captain Tanner," Bookman said, "what's his story? I take it he's not an actual uncle."

Ben looked at Tj, and she nodded. Doc and Bookman were family. Tj knew that she could trust them as much as she trusted Kyle, Jenna, Nikki, and Hunter. It seemed right to fill them in on what was going on, especially because Jordan Tanner would be around for the entire month of his leave.

"We have reason to believe that Captain Tanner— who wants us to call him Jordan, by the way—is Gracie's biological father," Tj informed the men. "It seems my mom had a one-night fling that happened to coincide with the time Gracie was conceived. My mom never told anyone that Gracie didn't belong to the man she was married to at the time, but somehow a friend of hers knew the truth and contacted Tanner after my mom died."

"I *can* see the resemblance," Bookman commented.

"Have you done any tests?" Doc asked.

"No. But he doesn't appear to want anything from us other than to get to know his daughter, so I didn't see any reason to rock the boat at this point. The only people who know why Jordan is here are Grandpa, Dad, Hunter, Jenna, Kyle, Nikki, and now the two of you. We'd like to keep it that way."

"The girls?" Bookman wondered.

"Think he's a friend of the family. He asked them to call him Uncle Jordan. We intentionally haven't told Helen or Bonnie what's really going on. I love them both, but there are no bigger gossips in town. I really don't want Gracie to find out. At least not at this point. I'm afraid it would just frighten and confuse her."

"We won't say a word," Bookman promised.

"And if you want to pursue testing, just let me know," Doc added. "I can make sure the whole thing is taken care of under the radar."

"Thanks." Tj hugged both men. "I'm not certain how this will play out, but I'm glad I have such good friends to go to if I need support."

"So other than setting up the sound system, what do you need us to do?" Ben asked.

"Jenna is coming by to help with the food, but I could use some help arranging the tables. I thought we'd set up some of those long conference tables along the front of the room to put the food on. And we have those big round tables in the storage room that easily can sit ten to twelve people each, so maybe we can set up three. we'll need folding chairs as well."

By the time Tj had finished giving the men instructions, Jenna had arrived, and the two women retreated to the kitchen to work on dinner. Tj was glad she and Jenna had something to keep themselves occupied with; it was evident they both were little more than bundles of nerves by that point.

"How did things go between your husband and his new daddy?" Tj teased.

"As predicted, Dennis blew a gasket. Bob left right away, but I'm afraid poor Bonnie had to deal with his temper for several hours before she finally up and left as well. Luckily, Mom kept the girls last night, so they don't realize anything is going on."

"The girls didn't come with you?"

"They're over at the house. I picked them up on my way here, and Mom was going to head over to Bonnie's to talk to her. I've done what I can with Dennis. When I left the house Josh was just pulling up, so I asked him to make sure Dennis made his way over here before dinner, and that he showed up sober. Josh is a good guy; if anyone can talk Dennis down it's him."

Tj turned the knob to preheat the industrial oven, which was large enough to cook all four turkeys at once. Sometimes it really was handy to live at a resort where you had a professional kitchen at your fingertips.

"The whole thing is such a mess," Jenna commented tiredly as she began making the dough for the rolls.

"Maybe once Dennis has a chance to think about things he'll cool down," Tj offered.

"I doubt it. Dennis really hates the guy, and I'm not sure I blame him. I was prepared to like him for Bonnie's sake, but there's something about him that I just don't trust."

Tj sighed. "I have to agree. I hoped for your sake and Bonnie's that he'd be really great, but I feel he has an end game of some sort, even though I can't figure out what it might be. Bonnie doesn't have a bunch of money I don't know about, does she? Because the guy seems to be exactly the sort I would suspect of being a gold digger."

Jenna put a towel over the dough to let it rise. It was going to take a lot of rolls to feed the crowd they expected.

"No," Jenna answered. "She owns her house and has a small savings plus a share in the Antiquery, but as far as I know that's it. She really has to watch her money most months. If he's looking for a gold mine, I'm afraid he's digging around in the wrong shaft."

Tj frowned. Something really wasn't adding up. Either *everyone* was reading the guy wrong or there was something going on that wasn't clearly evident. What would a wealthy, smooth-talking businessman want with Bonnie unless it really was love?

"If you're finished with the yams, you can start peeling the potatoes," Jenna instructed.

"I think we're going to have a *lot* of food," Tj commented.

"Yeah, I guess I went a bit overboard, considering some of our guests are bringing things, but focusing on the food took my mind off the Bonnie-and-Bob situation for short periods of time. We can send food home with everyone. How are things going with Uncle Jordan?"

"Better than I expected, which simultaneously terrifies and relieves me."

"Come again?" Jenna began assembling the ingredients for her famous broccoli casserole.

"At first I was terrified he was going to be some creep who would demand custody of Gracie in spite of the fact that it would destroy her sense of security and plunge her into a strange world filled with strange people. And when I met him and he seemed to be exactly what both you and Hunter assured me he would be—a nice guy who just wants to meet his daughter and has no intention of destroying her life— I began to relax. But the more I relax, the more terrified I get that he's planning to wait until my defenses are down and then move in for the kill."

"'Move in for the kill'?" Jenna laughed. "You've been watching too many dramas on TV. Kyle did a background check on the guy and he seems to be exactly what he says he is," she reminded Tj. "A background check! Why didn't I think about that before? I'll have Kyle do a background check on Bob King. Maybe if there's something to find, our super nerd can do it."

"Speaking of our super nerd, shouldn't he be here by now?" Tj wondered.

"He mentioned something about bringing Kiara and Annabeth early, so he probably had to go by his mom's to pick them up. I know Annabeth wanted to hang out with the girls and Kiara wanted to catch up with you. His mom is getting a ride with Frannie and her new boyfriend. They're also picking up Hazel."

"It's probably a good idea for people to car pool with the storm," Tj agreed.

"It looked like it was letting up when I drove over, but I have a feeling we're merely experiencing a pause and not an end to the storm. The plows were out, and your dad did a good job clearing the drive, so unless it really starts to dump, we should be okay. If we get snowed in, you have lots of empty cabins."

"How many of these potatoes do you think we need to peel?" Tj asked.

"All of them."

"I was afraid of that. You do realize that you can get mashed potatoes from a box? No peeling required."

Jenna made a face.

Tj returned to her chore.

"Do you think it's too early to turn on some Christmas music?" Jenna asked. "One of the radio stations is featuring around-the-clock holiday tunes."

"Music would be nice," Tj said. 'There's a radio on that shelf behind you."

Jenna turned on the music, then looked out the window at the snow. "It looks like Kyle and crew are here. Why don't you go say hi while I start on the pies?"

"Do you really think we need four different kinds of pie?"

"Probably not, but pumpkin is customary, Dennis likes chocolate cream, my mom prefers pecan, and I know your dad likes apple."

"Apple? You aren't making boysenberry?" Tj's face fell.

"You like pumpkin."

"I know, but I *love* boysenberry."

"I'll make you a boysenberry pie next week," Jenna promised. "Now go say hi to Annabeth and Kiara and send Kyle in to help me chop the veggies."

"What kind of veggies?"

"Carrots, asparagus, and cauliflower."

"And broccoli?" Tj asked hopefully.

"There's broccoli in the casserole."

"I know, but I like plain broccoli."

"Okay, I'll chop some broccoli and grill it in the oven."

"With chopped garlic?"

"With chopped garlic," Jenna confirmed. "Now scoot, before the kitchen is invaded and we have to figure out a tactful way of getting everyone out."

Chapter 5

"Everything looks so great," Nikki commented as she nibbled on one of Jenna's sausage and mushroom appetizers several hours later. Jenna really had outdone herself in the appetizer department. There were enough choices to make a meal.

Kallie agreed. "I really need to get the recipe for this dip. What's in it that gives it that kick? Is that horseradish?"

"You'll have to ask Jenna," Tj said. "She organized all the food; I just chopped and stirred as directed." Tj picked up a crab-filled wanton to nibble on. Everything really did look wonderful. Jenna might be distracted by the drama going on around her, but it apparently hadn't affected her cooking ability.

"I noticed Jenna's girls had on new dresses," Kallie added. "They look adorable. My mom always made me a new dress for the holidays when I was little. I wonder where she got that fabric. I love the fall colors in the print."

"I'm pretty sure Jenna said she made them with fabric she got the last time she was at the mall in the valley," Nikki replied. "I can barely handle a simple hem, but Jenna is a fantastic seamstress. I even heard she made those cool shirts for Dennis's bowling team. Speaking of Dennis, where is he? I haven't seen him since I've been here."

"He's coming later with Josh and Captain Brown," Tj answered.

"How did things go with Bonnie and her new guy?" Nikki asked.

While the situation with Jordan was a secret, most people in town knew that Bonnie had become engaged to a man no one had ever met. It had been the hot topic on the Serenity gossip lines for weeks.

"Not well," Tj admitted. "There were more fireworks in the Elston household yesterday than there were in last summer's July Fourth extravaganza over the lake. I'm hoping we don't have an encore today. Have either of you seen Bonnie?"

Kallie looked around the room. "I don't see her. Maybe she stepped out for some fresh air."

"It's freezing outside," Nikki pointed out.

"I haven't seen Bob all day. Bonnie may have gone over to his cabin to fetch him," Tj offered. "It really is rude of him to be so late when he knows Bonnie is here waiting."

"It does seem odd that the guy would come all the way to Serenity to see her and then totally ignore her once he got here," Nikki agreed. "Maybe he's having second thoughts about the engagement now that he's met her family. Dennis can be pretty formidable when he's upset about something."

"Yeah, maybe," Tj said.

"I think I'm going to go see if Jenna needs help," Kallie told them. "If I don't move away from this dip, I'm not going to be able to eat my dinner."

"Okay. Tell her to holler if she needs me," Tj called after her.

"Kallie seems to be sort of fidgety today," Nikki observed as Kallie left the room. "Is she nervous about something?"

"I suspect there may be a situation with her family," Tj answered. "She hasn't said anything, but originally she was really excited to have two weeks off to go home for a visit, and then all of a sudden she told me her plans had changed and she was staying in the area. I could sense a feeling of genuine distress."

"And you didn't ask her about it?"

"I don't know her well enough to nose around in her life."

Nikki laughed. "Who are you kidding? You nose around in everyone's life."

"Yeah," Tj admitted, "I guess I do. But in this case it didn't seem appropriate, and I've been pretty distracted with my own life drama."

Nikki picked up a stuffed mushroom and plopped it into her mouth. "And how is that life drama working out?"

"So far, so good. I'm not quite ready to let my guard down completely, but it appears Captain Tanner genuinely just wants to spend the holiday with Gracie before heading back out to sea."

"I'm sure you're right." Nikki gave Tj a quick hug. "If you need me for any reason, you know you can call me day or night."

"I know. And thanks. I would never have been able to deal with all this uncertainty without the support of my friends."

"Oh, hey, there's Bonnie." Nikki pointed across the room. "She just came in the front door. It looks like she's headed over to speak to Helen, Hazel, and Frannie."

Tj looked across the room where she'd last seen Helen holding court with all of the other hens in town. If you tossed in Harriet Kramer, you'd have the core of the Serenity gossip society. Everyone paused in their conversation to greet Bonnie, who looked flushed, as if she had just undergone some strenuous physical activity.

"So if Bonnie is talking to Helen, Hazel, and Frannie, where is her date?" Tj wondered as she watched the group. "You would think that if she was at his cabin fetching him, he would have come back with her."

"I don't know. I've never met the man, so I'm not sure what he looks like, but I didn't see anyone walk in with Bonnie. Maybe he wasn't ready and told her that he'd meet her here."

There was something nagging at Tj about the entire situation with Bob King. He didn't seem to be acting like a man in love. In fact, it didn't seem like he'd spent any time at all with his new fiancée since he'd arrived.

"So how is everything?" Jenna asked as she walked up behind them.

"Delicious," Nikki gushed.

"I'm ready to start serving dinner whenever everyone gets here."

"I think we're just missing a few people," Tj said. "Where's Kallie?"

"I haven't seen her," Jenna answered.

Tj frowned. "She said she was going to go help you in the kitchen."

Jenna picked up a radish and began to nibble on it. "I guess she got distracted. I didn't need the help anyway; other than finishing browning the rolls, we're good to go. Kyle sliced the turkey and Bookman mashed the potatoes. Doc is fussing with the gravy as we speak. He swears he has a secret recipe; knowing Doc, most likely that translates to hot, so be careful when you taste it."

"If Doc and Bookman are helping you, where's Grandpa?" Tj asked.

"He was out helping your dad with the snow, but I just saw them heading this way, so I think almost everyone should be here." Jenna looked around the room. "Where's Bob?"

"I haven't seen him," Tj said. "I'll go knock on his door to let him know we're almost ready to eat."

"I'll go with you," Nikki offered. "If I don't stop eating all of these fabulous appetizers, I'm not going to have room for dinner."

"It looks like Pastor Dan just walked in with Bren and Hannah. I guess I should go say hi," Jenna announced. "And I'll stop to grab a drink from the bar on my way over. It looks like it's time for the cook to relax and join the party."

"Grandpa and the guys mixed the rum punch, so it's bound to be strong."

"I tried the punch," Nikki commented. "From this point forward, I'm sticking with wine."

"Personally, right now I'm thinking the stronger the better," Jenna countered.

Tj watched as Jenna made her way across the room. It seemed everyone in attendance stopped her to tell her how fantastic her appetizers were. Jenna would be lucky to make her way to the bar before it was time to start serving dinner.

"It looks like Hazel is waving to you," Nikki said to Tj. "I'll knock on the guest of honor's door while you say hi."

Tj shrugged. "Okay, thanks. He's in cabin two."

Tj kept her eye on the room as she chatted with Hazel, and after an appropriate amount of time excused herself to say hi to Bren, who had been left standing alone after Dan wandered away to speak to Hunter and Jenna returned to the kitchen.

"So did you meet Bonnie's new guy?" Bren asked.

"Yeah. Did you?"

"Unfortunately. I very unwisely decided to stop by Jenna's yesterday and walked into the middle of Armageddon. I don't think I've ever seen Dennis quite that irate."

"Poor Bonnie. What was Bob doing while Dennis was tearing into him?" Tj wondered.

"Drinking Dennis's scotch. The guy seems like a real toad. I don't know what Bonnie sees in him."

"Yeah, I'm afraid toad is the consensus. Did you happen to see him walking around outside when you drove up from the road? I sent Nikki to his cabin, but she said he didn't answer when she knocked on his door. We're still waiting for a couple of other guests, but the food is ready and I think Jenna is anxious to start serving."

"I saw him outside by the woodshed, talking to Captain Brown."

Tj frowned. "I didn't think Captain Brown and the others were here yet."

"I didn't see Josh or Dennis, but Brown is here with the fire truck. Maybe Dennis and Josh headed over to the house. Actually, here they are now."

Tj looked where Bren was pointing. Dennis had walked in with Josh and Captain Brown on his heels, but there was no sign of Bob King. Maybe Captain Brown had convinced him to keep his distance from Dennis for everyone's sake. Tj certainly hoped so. In fact, it wouldn't be the worst thing in the world if Bob decided to stay in his cabin and skip dinner altogether.

"It looks like Bonnie is going over to talk to Dennis. Should we intervene? Or maybe get Jenna?"

Tj watched as Bonnie said something to Dennis. He appeared to be listening to her request because he nodded before he ordered a drink. Bonnie went back to Hazel, who was sitting alone at the table. Tj noticed that Frannie's date was chatting with Helen near the bar, so maybe Frannie had gone to the ladies' room to freshen up.

"So far, so good." Hunter walked up and put his arm around Tj.

"Yeah. I can't believe we've managed to avoid having any fireworks. Where's Jake?"

"Talking to your grandpa, Doc, and Bookman. I'm afraid my grandfather is trying to convince Doc to be our next mayor."

"What? Doc would never want to be mayor. He hates following the rules. Besides, being mayor is a full-time job. Doc is retired. I don't think he's looking for full-time work."

"I have to agree, but Grandpa heard that a couple members of the council have been talking about looking for a mayor from out of the area. Jake thinks that's a mistake. He's actually proposing hiring a town manager to do the grunt work and making the position of mayor a part-time position that can be fulfilled by a local business owner, or maybe a retiree."

"I like Jake's idea, but Doc will never do it. You need to find someone who loves the town, has the time, and is likely to want to play by the rules. Someone like you." Tj grinned.

"Trust me, I don't have the time. What about your dad?"

Tj thought about it. "I doubt he has the time either. Jenna is waving at me; I should get back to the kitchen."

"I'll help," Hunter offered.

"I'd like to make a toast," Mike began a short while later, after everyone had gathered around and the food had been set out on the buffet tables in preparation for the big feast. "To family, friends, and neighbors. I feel so blessed to share this very snowy holiday with you all. Dig in and enjoy."

"Short and sweet," Hunter whispered to Tj.

"Dad isn't really a speech sort of guy. In fact, I'm surprised he said anything at all. My guess is that Rosalie nudged him into it."

"It seems like they're getting pretty serious," Hunter said.

"Yes and no. They spend a lot of time together, but she never stays over, and Dad is home every night, so I know he doesn't stay with her. If I had to guess, I'd say they've settled into a comfortable companionship. It's hard to tell at this point if it will develop into more."

"Would you care if it did?" Hunter wondered.

Tj thought about it. "No. I really like Rosalie. If at some point she and Dad decided to get married, I'd be happy for them both."

"It looks like your dinner is a success," Kyle said as the people seated at the table closest to the food— Ashley, Gracie, Kristi, Kari, Jordan, Kiara, Annabeth, Bren, Dan, Hannah, and Kyle's mom, Vicki—got up and began filling their plates.

"It looks like your mom is enjoying sitting with the kids," Tj commented as she watched them. "Is she enjoying being a mom to Annabeth?"

"She really is. I'm not sure why she didn't have a houseful of children. She always has been drawn to them. And, thankfully, with Annabeth to mother, she's stopped smothering me."

"Come on now; your mom is a doll. I bet you at least miss the hot cocoa before bed since she moved into her own place." Tj grinned.

"Okay, I guess I miss the attention at times, but I don't miss her doing my laundry or throwing away all my junk food. The entire time she lived with me, I had to hide a stash of chips and candy bars in my bedroom closet."

Tj laughed. "That *would* be a drag." She turned to Jenna, who seemed to be staring into space. "Are you okay?"

"I was just wondering how the conversation is going over at the table where Bob is seated. It looks like Bonnie has a scowl on her face that seems to become more and more pronounced the longer he talks. I find myself hoping all is not well in love land and Bob will go home early and never return."

Tj looked to the table Bob shared with Bonnie, Ben, Doc, Bookman, Helen, Jake, Mike, Rosalie, and Hazel. "She does look pretty irritated," Tj agreed, "but I hope the lack of fireworks we've enjoyed so far continues for another couple of hours at least."

"At least Dennis seems content to stay out of things," Kyle said.

Dennis, Josh, and Captain Brown were eating at the bar.

"Looks like our table is up next," Frannie announced.

Tj followed Frannie as she stood up along with her date, Kyle, Jenna, Hunter, Kallie, and Nikki.

"I'm afraid I may have enjoyed too many of your appetizers to do justice to the fantastic dinner you prepared," Nikki said to Jenna.

"You can always take home some leftovers and heat them up later," Jenna suggested. "I have a feeling we're going to have a ton of food left."

"I had a bite of the turkey before you brought it out," Kallie said. "It really is delicious. Did you baste it in something other than its own juice?"

"Butter," Jenna told her. "Lots and lots of real butter."

"My waistline might not appreciate that, but my taste buds certainly do."

After everyone had filled their plates they returned to the table and ate in silence. Tj noticed that Jenna was picking at the food on her plate but not really eating it.

"Is something wrong?" Tj whispered.

"Not really. I guess I'm just waiting for the other shoe to drop."

"Relax," Tj encouraged. "Nothing bad has happened so far, which means nothing bad is likely to happen."

Jenna didn't look up.

"Is something else wrong?"

Jenna finally looked up and glanced around the table.

"Don't worry; the guys are all talking football, Kallie and Nikki are swapping recipes, and Frannie and her date went back for seconds. No one is paying any attention to our conversation."

"It's just that it's Thanksgiving and I haven't spent any time with my husband," Jenna said softly.

"So go talk to him."

Jenna looked toward the bar and frowned. "Did you see where he went?"

Tj looked around the room. "He's talking to his mother." Tj nodded toward the table where Dennis was sitting next to Bonnie. They appeared to be chatting politely. Bob had gotten up from his seat, most likely to refill his plate, although Tj didn't see him at the buffet table either.

"I hate to interrupt his conversation with his mom. Maybe once Bob gets back I'll go over to see if he's in the mood to spend some time with his wife."

Tj couldn't help but notice that Jenna sounded bitter. The entire situation must be wearing on her more than she was letting on.

"Should we think about putting out the desserts?" Tj asked.

"Maybe. It looks like most people are finishing up."

Frannie returned to the table minus her date and minus the food Tj had thought she'd gone to get. "I'm afraid Arnie and I have to leave. I've been battling a headache all day and even though I've taken aspirin, I can't seem to shake it."

"I'm sorry to hear that." Tj stood up. "Can we send you off with a doggy bag? Maybe some pie?"

"Thanks, but I really need to get going." Frannie seemed almost frantic to leave, which was odd since she hadn't said anything about having a headache earlier.

"Hazel came with us and I hate to ask her to leave early. Can someone give her a ride?" Frannie asked.

"We'll see that she gets home," said Kyle, who had just tuned into the conversation.

Kallie stood up and hugged Frannie. "I'm going to run to the ladies' room. If you're gone by the time I get back, it was nice talking to you."

"You too, dear. And do remember to come by for that book we discussed."

"I will. Drive safely."

Jenna got up also. "Captain Brown just said something to Dennis. They both stepped outside. I think I'm going to try to intercept Dennis when he comes back in to see if he wants to talk. Is it okay if we go over to your house, where we can have some privacy?"

"Absolutely. Go on, and I'll start serving the pies."

In all, there were twelve pies for thirty people. Not only had Jenna made eight, two each of the four types she had prepared, but several other guests had brought pies as well. There was one thing for certain: no one was going to leave hungry.

"Can I help?" Helen walked into the kitchen.

"Thanks. I'd appreciate it."

"Where did Jenna go off to?" her mother asked.

"She went to look for Dennis."

"Captain Brown came in and told him that he needed to respond to a call," Helen informed her. "Dennis walked him out, but I'm sure he planned to come right back in. He didn't even take his jacket."

"Did Josh go with him?"

"They both left," Helen confirmed. "For a minute I thought Dennis might make an excuse to try to go with them, but he didn't say that was his plan. He seems to be doing better now than he was yesterday. Of course, I think Josh managed to get a few drinks into him, which I'm sure helped, and Bob has made himself scarce for most of the day, although I think Bonnie feels put out that Bob hasn't spent more time with her."

"Did he indicate why he hadn't?" Tj asked. It did seem odd that he'd been away from the party for such long periods of time.

"No, not really. When we first arrived at the resort he seemed happy to see Bonnie. We were walking from the parking area toward the activities room when Frannie pulled up with Arnie, Hazel, and Vicki. I went over to say hi to the new arrivals, and when I returned to where I'd left Bonnie and Bob, she informed me that Bob had gone back to get something he'd left in his room, so we continued on without him. It was over an hour before he finally showed up. He had dinner with us, excused himself to go to the men's room, and I haven't seen him since."

"Maybe he isn't feeling well but doesn't want to say so."

"Maybe. Do you have serving utensils for this many pies?"

Tj opened a few drawers to take a quick inventory of what she had on hand. "It looks like I didn't bring enough over from the Grill, but I can run over to get a few more. Why don't you go ahead and set out the pies we have servers for and I'll be back in a jiffy."

Tj looked around the room as she made her way from the small kitchen in the activities room toward the back entrance, which led to a path connecting the building to the Grill. She didn't see either Dennis or

Jenna, so she hoped they were at the house, working things out. She hated to see Jenna so miserable, especially during a dinner she'd worked so hard to provide for her friends and family. It was a shame that neither Elston had been able to enjoy the exquisite meal.

Tj pulled on her heavy boots, down jacket, hat, and gloves before she plowed her way through the drifts, which were thigh-high in some places. It looked like she was going to be in for a good workout the next day. With the staff on vacation, it was up to her and her dad to keep the walkways clear, although she was sure if she asked, Kyle would help out as well.

She decided to cut across the forest since the walkways weren't clear anyway and the forest trail was shorter. She had almost reached the Grill when she tripped and fell over something buried in the snow.

"What the . . ." She grabbed her ankle as she tried to make out what it was she'd snagged her foot on. "Oh God," she groaned, just before she lost her dinner in the snow.

Chapter 6

"Is that the new deputy?" Kyle whispered to Tj as they waited for the guests who were still at the resort to be interviewed.

The *something* Tj had tripped on had been a body; Bob King's body, to be exact. Someone had buried the body in the snow, but the worst part was that the prime suspect was the man who would have been his son-in-law.

"He's a deputy from Indulgence, on loan for the holiday weekend," Tj whispered back. "He certainly isn't as sweet and cuddly as Dylan. Here I am, traumatized by tripping over a very dead body, and all he does is grill me as if I'd killed the guy. If Hunter hadn't stepped in, I might have decked him, and then they would have had two inmates in the Serenity jail tonight."

"You don't think Dennis really . . ." Kyle left the sentence unfinished.

"God, I hope not, but Dennis *was* missing when Jenna and I looked for him after he spoke to Bonnie, which wasn't all that long before Jenna went looking for him and I tripped over the body. I know he loathed the guy, but I can't believe Dennis would kill anyone."

"He's really protective of the women in his family," Kyle pointed out.

"Yeah, he is."

Tj sat quietly, dreading what was to come. It was going to take forever to interview everyone. Frannie and her date, Arnie, had already left by the time Tj called the sheriff, and Hazel had decided to go with them. Pastor Dan and Bren had taken Hannah home, and Kallie wasn't around, so Tj assumed she'd left as well. Captain Brown and Josh had been called to respond to an emergency before she'd found the body, and Hunter had managed to talk the deputy into allowing the kids under twelve to return to the house, with Annabeth to supervise. They'd escorted Bonnie out and taken Dennis into custody. Jenna had never returned to the party. That still left thirteen adults to interview, including Tj. Judging by the rate with which the man was moving, they were in for a long, long night.

"Do you know where Jenna is?" Helen wandered over to where Tj and Kyle were sitting in the back of the room.

"I haven't seen her. I know she was going to go find Dennis to try to talk to him. She was planning to go over to the house. I'm pretty sure that was where Dennis was found, but I don't know what happened to Jenna. Roy took Dennis into town," Tj said, referring to Roy Fisher, the acting lead detective until the sheriff could find a replacement for Dylan. "She might still be at the house, or I suppose Roy might have let her go into town with her husband. I doubt she'd leave without making sure the girls were okay, but she *did* know that we were here to see to them."

"My poor, poor baby."

"You don't think Dennis . . ." Tj asked Helen the same question Kyle had asked her.

"No. Dennis loves his mother. I don't think he would cause her this amount of pain, no matter how much he disliked her new boyfriend."

"Where is Bonnie anyway?"

"She left with Tim. I haven't seen her since."

Tim Matthews was the junior deputy assigned to the town of Serenity.

"At least they're letting people leave once they've been interviewed," Helen commented.

"Yeah, but it's been two hours, and so far the only people who've been allowed to leave are Vicki Donovan and Nikki Weston. I guess they allowed Kiara to go to help Annabeth, which leaves ten of us. They're talking to Rosalie right now and they've already talked to me, although they warned me to stay put. They seem to be listening to Hunter, so chances are they don't suspect him, so his interview may go quickly. Why don't you go next?" Tj suggested to Helen. "You can make sure Kristi and Kari get home."

"Okay. I'll bring Ashley and Gracie with me and drop Vicki, Kiara, and Annabeth at home as well."

"Thanks, I appreciate it. If you hear from Jenna, call me."

"I will," Helen promised. "And if you hear from her, you call me."

Although the interviews seemed to move along at a glacial speed, eventually there was just Tj, Kyle, and Hunter left. Mike and Ben had retired to the house, and Tj suspected that Doc, Bookman, and Jake were still waiting with them. Hunter and Kyle had both been interviewed, but they'd refused to leave until the deputy released Tj as well.

"Tell me again how you happened across Mr. King's body," the borrowed deputy asked for the fourth time.

"I told you: I was in the kitchen with Helen Henderson and we realized we needed additional utensils to serve the pies, so I volunteered to go over to the Grill to get some."

"Helen is the suspect's mother-in-law?"

"Yes," Tj groaned. "You know that. Why do you keep asking the same questions over and over?"

"And the suspect—where was he at that time?" the deputy asked, totally disregarding Tj's complaint.

"I'm not really sure, but I believe he was at the house. I know Jenna intended to track him down to take him over to the house so they could have a chat."

"A chat about what?" the man asked.

Tj wanted to say that it was none of his business, but she realized that would only delay the interview. "Jenna was feeling sad that she hadn't had much time to spend with her husband. It *is* a holiday."

"And how long before you stumbled across Mr. King's body had Mrs. Elston left the building?"

Tj signed. Her headache was going to turn into a migraine if this annoying man didn't wrap things up soon. "I don't know. Maybe half an hour. I was busy. There was a lot going on and I wasn't watching the time."

The borrowed deputy jotted down some notes. Tj hoped the pause in his questioning meant that he was wrapping things up. He went so far as to put his pen back into his shirt pocket before he asked the next question.

"And when did you first notice that Mr. Elston was missing?"

Tj glanced at Hunter. She hoped he could see the desperation in her eyes and would back her up if she strangled the man.

"Shortly before Jenna left to look for him," Tj answered. "He was talking to his mother, and then Captain Brown came in to tell him that he needed to respond to a call, and Dennis walked him out. I didn't see him again after that, so I assume Jenna found him and they went to talk. Do we have to go over all of this again? I'm beyond tired."

The borrowed deputy hesitated before replying. "I guess I can interview you again at another time if you agree to two stipulations."

"Anything."

"One, you don't leave the area, and two, you stay out of this investigation."

Tj looked shocked that he'd say that.

"Your reputation precedes you, Ms. Jensen. Do we have a deal?"

Tj hesitated. Could she agree to that? Dennis needed her. Jenna needed her.

"Well?"

"Okay, I agree."

"Fine; then you're free to go."

After the borrowed deputy left, Kyle and Hunter helped Tj store the leftover food in the large refrigerator in the Grill; no use wasting what amounted to hundreds of dollars' worth of perfectly good food. Tj called her dad, who informed her that Doc, who was a retired coroner who occasionally helped out when the county needed him, Jake, a retired doctor and the founder of Serenity Community Hospital, and Bookman, a famous author and town council member, were using their connections to get any information they could on both the victim and the suspect. Tj had left numerous messages on Jenna's phone, but so far she hadn't called back. Tj's heart bled for her.

"This whole thing is surreal," Kyle commented as he covered the untouched pies with plastic wrap.

"I know it looks like Dennis killed Bob, but I can't bring myself to believe he would actually hurt *anyone*," Tj said.

"Maybe he didn't," Hunter countered. "There were thirty people in the building. I suppose anyone in attendance had the opportunity to kill the man."

"Yeah, but who else would *want* to kill Bob?" Tj asked.

"There was something really off about that guy," Kyle said. "Maybe he had enemies we don't know about."

"In Serenity? Among our friends and family?" Tj questioned.

"I guess it's unlikely that one of the other guests did it," Kyle admitted. "Still, I find that I'm curious about the real Bob King."

"Maybe you should dig around," Hunter suggested.

"I promised I wouldn't," Tj reminded him.

"True, but Kyle didn't. How about it? Want to see what you can pull up on the man behind the phony smile?"

Kyle grinned. "Actually, I would."

"Why don't you go ahead and head over to the house? Tj and I will finish up and then join you. Maybe we can figure this out without getting Tj in trouble for breaking her promise to the deputy. I hate to admit it, but he seems about as clueless as they come."

"I know. Did you hear how he kept asking the same questions over and over?" Tj commented.

"While repetition is an interrogation tactic, I think he just forgot what he'd already asked," Hunter agreed.

"And see if you can find out what happened to Jenna," Tj instructed Kyle as he put on his coat to head over to the house.

"So how are you holding up?" Hunter pulled Tj into his arms for a tight hug after Kyle left.

"I'm hanging in. I just feel so bad for Jenna and Dennis. And poor Bonnie. Bob seemed like a real jerk, but she seemed to care for him. She must be devastated."

Hunter kissed Tj on the forehead and then took a step back to return to his job of wrapping leftovers to store them in the commercial refrigerator in the Grill. "And how are things going with Uncle Jordan?" he asked.

"Great. He's really good with the girls and they seem to love him already. I just hope the guy is as genuine as he seems. I have to be honest: I'm still having a hard time relaxing about the whole thing."

"Understandable. Do you want to save the leftover veggies? They might make good soup."

"Save everything unless it's perishable and has been sitting out for an extended period," Tj suggested. "I'll let Kallie sort out what to save and what to toss."

"I think we should call time of death on these wontons," Hunter said. "The cream cheese filling might have gone bad by now."

"I really am glad you were here today," Tj said. "That borrowed deputy seemed like he was going to be a real problem until you stepped in and organized things."

"Happy to help." Hunter smiled.

"Do you remember that Thanksgiving when we were seniors in high school?"

"I talked you into coming to my house to meet my aunts and uncles, who were visiting from Boston."

"Hands down the worst Thanksgiving of my life up to and including this one," Tj declared.

Hunter laughed. "It wasn't that bad."

"Really? Your mom spent the entire afternoon pointing out every one of my faults, real or imagined, to anyone and everyone who would listen. You were so busy watching football with your dad and uncles that you didn't even notice. Chelsea was upstairs pouting all afternoon because some guy she had invited didn't show, and I was left alone in the wolves' den with your mom and aunts."

"I'm really sorry." Hunter sounded sincere. "I guess I wasn't a very good boyfriend back then."

"You weren't *that* bad," Tj said. "You just had blinders on when it came to the fact that your mom hated me from the moment we started dating."

"She didn't hate you."

Tj rolled her eyes. "Don't tell me that after everything she's done to keep us apart you still believe that? The woman broke us up!"

Hunter stopped what he was doing and came across the room to where Tj was standing. He took her hand in his and turned so that he faced her. "My mistakes were my mistakes. I was young and immature, and I freely admit I was a jerk. Yes, my mom wanted to see me marry someone she considered to be in our 'social class,' but in the end I was the one who let you go. I've regretted it every day since. If I get another chance with you, I promise I won't let that happen again."

Tj wanted to say something, but she honestly had no idea what it was. She'd loved Hunter ever since she'd met him, but he'd hurt her, and she wasn't sure she wanted to trust him with her heart again.

"It looks like we're done here," Hunter announced. "How about we go find out what, if anything, Kyle might have discovered?"

"Yeah, okay. You get the lights and I'll lock the back door."

Hunter and Tj walked through the snow from the activities room to the house. It was snowing hard enough that the walkways Mike had shoveled were covered with fresh powder.

"The house looks nice," Hunter said.

Her dad and grandpa had begun the holiday decorating by stringing lights along the eaves.

"It's a start. You should see the plans Grandpa has for the rest of the resort. It's really going to be like living in Santa's Village."

"Santa's Village is one of my favorite places." Hunter grinned.

Tj smiled back. "Mine too."

They had first gotten together at Santa's Village. Hunter, as football captain, and Tj, as cheerleading captain, had been selected to play Mr. and Mrs. Claus at the annual team fund-raiser. At first, neither had wanted to do it, but by the end of the evening their status as a couple had been firmly in place.

Tj hung up her coat as the pair entered the house through the kitchen. Each placed their wet boots in the mudroom and slipped on a pair of the heavy socks her grandfather kept laundered and available for whoever might need something warm for their feet. Tj tossed another log on the kitchen fire before joining the others in the living area of the large home.

"So what have we learned?" Tj asked.

"Dennis has been charged with first-degree murder and Jenna has been charged as an accessory," Kyle informed the newcomers.

"Jenna is in jail?" Tj exploded.

Echo ran to her side, looking at her anxiously. It was obvious he sensed her distress but didn't have a clue as to the cause.

"It's okay," Tj assured him. She scratched his head and then asked him to lie down. "What happened?" she asked in a much calmer tone of voice.

"I guess when the deputies showed up they went to the house looking for Dennis. Jenna told them that he wasn't there," Kyle answered.

"Oh God. She lied to protect him," Tj realized.

"If she lied to protect him, she must have thought he was guilty," Kyle pointed out. "It really does look like he might have done this."

"Maybe he did, maybe he didn't. Maybe Jenna just panicked when she realized that something was going on and the cops were looking for her husband. Either way, we have to get her out of jail."

"I'm ready to post bail the minute they set it," Kyle assured her. "The problem is that since it's a holiday weekend, they're saying bail won't be set until she can see the judge on Monday."

"We can't leave her there until Monday," Tj insisted.

"I'll call Judge Harper," Hunter volunteered.

"Already did," Jake joined in. "He's no longer a sitting judge, but he's going to use his influence to see what he can do."

Tj put her hands over her face as she sank into the sofa behind her. Echo put his head in her lap and she mindlessly scratched him behind the ears. "I can't believe this is happening."

"Don't worry." Her dad sat down next to her and put his arm around her. "We'll figure this out."

Tj looked around the room. The people she trusted most to do just that were all there: her dad, her grandfather, Bookman, Doc, Jake, Kyle, and Hunter. If she were going to assemble a team to help her help Jenna and Dennis, this was exactly who she'd call on.

"Has anyone called Helen?" Tj asked.

"No, it didn't occur to us," her dad said.

"I'll do it right now." Tj dialed Helen's home number and waited. Poor Helen was going to freak when she found out Jenna was in jail. The entire situation was insane.

"Hello?" said a deep, masculine voice.

"Jordan?" Tj asked when someone who sounded exactly like their guest answered Helen's phone. "What are you doing at Helen's?"

"The girls were pretty hysterical by the time Helen rounded them up to take them home, so I offered to help out. It took a while, but we managed to get them to bed. I thought about calling a cab and heading back to the resort, but Bren and Helen are kind of hysterical themselves, so I decided to stay for a bit. Have your heard from Jenna?"

Jordan was calming down hysterical women and children? Somehow the image of the huge and formidable man comforting them didn't fit. Still, the girls seemed to love him, and he did have a way about him that let you know he was in control of a situation. Maybe he was the perfect man for the job. Tj decided to fill in Jordan and let him break the news to Helen. He was handling things well to this point, and he'd been in combat. He could certainly handle one tiny, hysterical woman.

"And the worst part is that since it's a holiday weekend, we're being told Jenna's bail won't be set until Monday," Tj finished.

"I can stay here as long as I need to," Jordan assured Tj. "If there's anything more I can do, just let me know."

"Okay, that's actually very helpful." Tj hung up.

"Did Jordan say anything about Bonnie?" Ben asked.

"I forgot to ask. No one has heard from her?"

Everyone confirmed that they hadn't.

"Maybe I can get hold of Tim or Roy. If I can catch them when they aren't within hearing distance of their new boss, they'll probably fill me in on what's going on."

After leaving several messages, Tj did finally get hold of Roy while he was driving home for the night. When she asked about Bonnie, his answer sent a chill of fear to the very core of her being.

"What do you mean, she's missing?" Ben asked after Tj had hung up with Roy and begun filling in the men in the room. "I thought she left with one of the deputies."

"Roy says she left with Tim, who took her down to the station. Tim left her alone in his office to get her a cup of coffee. When he came back she was gone. No one saw her leave."

"Why would she just leave like that?" Tj asked.

"Roy indicated that she got some disturbing news regarding Mr. King that really flipped her out."

"What did she find out?" Ben asked.

"Roy wouldn't say," Tj told them.

"I think I might know," Kyle, who was sitting at the computer, said. "It appears Bob King is a small-time con artist who has swindled dozens of women out of their lives' savings. He's been married seven times in the past twenty years. In each case he convinced the women he married to open a joint savings account with him for the purpose of purchasing a dream home or a business for the couple to run together. Of course he would just disappear with the money and never complete the sale of the property."

"Poor Bonnie." Doc shook his head.

"I knew there was something off about the guy, but Jenna said Bonnie didn't have any money," Tj commented. "Or at least not enough to attract a swindler."

"Maybe she had money Jenna didn't know about, or King just thought she did. Either way, it appears he was after something other than true love," Kyle stated.

"We really need to find Bonnie," Ben said. "She must be beside herself."

"And we need to get Jenna out of jail," Tj added.

"I'll get it," Mike said when the house phone rang.

"How about I take you home?" Hunter said to Jake. His grandfather had a sharp mind, but he was getting on in years and his health hadn't been all that great as of late.

"As soon as we hear from Judge Harper," he promised. "I won't be able to sleep, not knowing whether Jenna is going to be released. That poor girl. Any fool can see she should be home with her young daughters."

"This entire situation really is crazy," Kyle agreed. "Maybe the call Mike went to answer was from Judge Harper. If Harper doesn't have any luck getting Jenna released I'll hire the best attorney I can find and try to approach things from a different direction. I doubt the borrowed deputy has enough to hold her for any length of time. Chances are he's just trying to wear her down so she'll implicate her husband."

"The question is, could an attorney, even a good one, do much tonight?" Tj asked.

"Probably not," Kyle admitted. "But a good attorney could get her released in the morning, not make her wait until the courts open on Monday."

"That was Judge Harper on the phone," Mike confirmed as he returned to the room. "Both Dennis and Jenna have been released. Tim is taking them home."

"They let Dennis go as well?" Tj asked. "Why?"

"Because someone else came in and confessed to the murder."

"Someone else confessed?" Ben asked. "Who?"

"Bonnie," Tj realized.

Chapter 7

Tuesday, December 2

Once Tj confirmed that Dennis and Jenna were home safely, everyone said their good-byes and went home.

No one actually thought Bonnie had killed the man she was engaged to, although everyone agreed she seemed to have a good motive to do so. Tj suspected Bonnie had simply confessed to the murder in order to get both Dennis and Jenna out of jail. Her intention might have been noble, but her confession gave the borrowed deputy a reason to consider the case closed, which, on one hand, was good because it sent him home to Indulgence; on the other hand, it was bad because now no one was looking for the real killer.

Once the courts opened on Monday, Kyle arranged for Bonnie to get out on bail, so everyone Tj loved was safe and accounted for, at least for the time being. Roy had secretly told Tj that neither he nor Tim believed Bonnie had actually killed Bob King and would continue to dig around under the radar, even though the sheriff seemed content to let things be.

The Christmas tree lighting in the town square had been postponed, partly due to the uproar caused by the murder and partly because of all the snow that had fallen the previous day. Once the sun had come out, much of the snow melted, so the new date had been set for Friday. So much had happened in just a few short days, yet the town seemed to be back to normal, its citizens refocused on Christmas and everything that went along with that magical time of year.

Tj had spent some time considering the situation and discussing options with both Jenna and Kyle, but there wasn't much that could be done in the short term, so Tj went about her normal routine, planning and implementing preholiday chores. The resort reopened as planned on the Saturday after Thanksgiving, and with fresh snow on the slopes, they'd been booked to capacity ever since. She'd barely seen her dad since the masses arrived, and sightings of her grandpa were slim as well. Surprisingly, Jordan had jumped right in to help out where he could. He spent his days doing whatever seemed to need to be done, and when the girls came home after school and extracurricular activities, he all but took over their care and supervision. He really did seem to be cut out to be a dad. To some other child. Tj would never give up custody of Gracie without a fight, but if Jordan wanted to visit whenever he was in port, Tj was beginning to recognize that perhaps his presence in her sister's life was a good thing rather than a bad one.

Jenna had closed the Antiquery over the weekend but had reopened on Monday with both Helen and Bonnie's help. Bren was working at the restaurant fewer hours than she once had given the fact that she seemed to have moved into the role of full-time nanny for Pastor Dan and Hannah. Dan tended to be home on weekday mornings, so Bren filled in at the Antiquery when she could.

Tj knew that Kyle had been at the high school that day, working with the choir. Since the date of the tree lighting and choral recital had been changed, and there was no longer a conflict with the various Thanksgiving plans of her students' families, the number of students willing to participate had almost doubled. Perhaps moving the tree lighting up a week on a permanent basis wouldn't be a bad idea. Tj decided she'd talk to the new mayor about it, if they ever actually got around to choosing a new mayor.

"Seems like things are back to normal," Tj commented when Jenna took a break during play practice and sat down next to her in the audience, where Tj had been watching the town's children rehearse their lines.

"If it weren't for the fact that there's a murder trial looming over our heads at some as-yet-to-be-determined point in the future, I'd totally agree."

"Have you made any headway with Bonnie?" Tj asked.

"Not really. We all know she didn't kill Bob King. We also know Dennis didn't do it, but the only reason Sheriff Boggs doesn't have Dennis in jail at this very minute is because of Bonnie's confession, so she won't recant it. There's really only one solution: we have to find the real killer."

"I promised I wouldn't interfere," Tj reminded Jenna.

Jenna just looked at her.

"But of course I will."

"Good." Jenna sighed with relief. "Annabeth, move a little to the left, and make sure all the baby angels are sitting behind the line," she directed from her seat.

"Maybe you should head back up since Kyle is tied up with the choir," Tj suggested.

"Yeah, maybe I should. Dennis is on administrative leave all week. Captain Brown thought it was best, given the situation. Even though Bonnie confessed, I think that in most people's minds Dennis is still the prime suspect."

"Paid leave?"

"Thankfully yes. I don't know what we'd do if the county refused to pay him. Anyway, he can watch the kids tonight if you want to meet after rehearsal to come up with a strategy. I spoke to Kyle, and he's on board to meet us wherever we decide."

"I'll need to take the girls home."

"Jordan is here," Jenna informed Tj. "He came in while you were on the phone outside. He's helping Kyle right now, but he said he'd be happy to give Ashley and Gracie a ride out to the resort. I guess he borrowed your dad's old pickup."

"Okay, I'm in. I haven't eaten all day. How about Rob's?"

"Sounds perfect. I'll call Dennis and have him come to get Kristi and Kari and confirm with Kyle." Jenna looked back toward the stage. "Do you think we should have Beth stand somewhere else? As the narrator, we don't want her to upstage the others, but I feel like she's too hidden in her current location."

"Have her sit on the bench the baby angels use in the last scene. It will make it seem like she's part of the action and yet somewhat removed from it."

"Good idea." Jenna stood up. "And thanks for helping me with the other."

"That's what friends are for."

After rehearsal wrapped up and all the young actors had been picked up by their parents, Tj, Jenna, and Kyle headed over to Rob's Pizza, a comfy joint with vinyl booths, red-checkered tablecloths, team pictures on the walls, video games, and the best pizza west of the Rockies.

Like most of the establishments in Serenity, Rob's was decked out for the holiday season. A life-size mechanical Santa stood next to a huge Christmas tree that occupied one corner of the room. Freshly cut fir branches had been fashioned into wreaths that were tied up with red and green bows and hung around the room. Even the large river-rock fireplace, which created a cozy feel on a cold winter day, had been decorated with red-and-white-striped stockings and tall red and white candles. Tj considered the menu as seasonal carols played on the old-fashioned jukebox.

After ordering an extra-large double combo pizza and a pitcher of beer, the trio dug right into the problem at hand.

"I've been doing some digging," Kyle began. "While there are large gaps in the history I'm putting together for our victim, it's apparent that his pattern was to meet women who were both wealthy and vulnerable, romance the socks off of them, convince them in a short period of time that he was Prince Charming come to sweep them off their feet, gain access to their money, and then disappear. He never invested more than six months in any one woman."

"He didn't seem all that charming," Tj pointed out. "I really can't see how he got all of those women to fall for him."

"It does appear there was something different going on on this occasion," Kyle acknowledged. "For one thing, I can't find any indication that Mr. King met the family of his other victims. He seemed to target women who were alone in the world and didn't have anyone to watch out for them Of course, I've only put together part of the story at this point, so we may find that he used different patterns in differing circumstances."

"How had he managed to keep doing this for twenty years? Shouldn't he have been in jail?" Tj asked.

Kyle pulled a sheet of paper out of his pocket. "According to what I could find, Bob King had been brought in for questioning quite a few times. In most cases he was let go, but I also found evidence that he served a few short sentences over the years. Several years ago he was involved in a hit-and-run accident while he was drunk. The arresting officer was new and made an error, so even though Bob was obviously guilty of killing a woman, who happened to be pregnant at the time, he was released after serving only a few short weeks behind bars."

"And these women?" Jenna asked. "He married them, took their money, and then what?"

"He divorced them, or they divorced him after he took off. There are also a few women I found reference to who he never married. He was engaged to them, stole their money, and then disappeared before they actually tied the knot."

"Do we know if he got any money from Bonnie?" Tj asked.

Kyle looked at Jenna.

"I don't know," she answered. "She's refusing to speak to either Dennis or me about the situation. We've tried to bring it up a few times and she completely shuts down. As long as we keep the subject matter focused on the kids or the upcoming holiday she seems fine, but the minute we mention the man she was engaged to, his murder, or her upcoming trial, she checks out completely."

The conversation paused as the waitress brought their pizza. "Rudolph, the Red-Nosed Reindeer" was playing on the jukebox as the three friends consumed their first pieces. Based on the way Kyle and Jenna dug into the cheesy pie, Tj realized she wasn't the only one who hadn't eaten much that day. Between her classes, downhill practice with her team, play rehearsal, helping out at the resort, and making holiday plans, Tj felt like she was caught in some sort of endless vortex. She didn't have time to investigate a murder, but she couldn't let Bonnie go to prison for a crime she hadn't committed either.

"Has Bonnie talked to the lawyer you hired?" Tj asked Jenna as she picked at the toppings from her second piece of the fully loaded pie.

"No. She refuses to speak to him. She won't explain to anyone what happened, and she won't say anything to defend herself. She's even refusing to share with the attorney the specifics of her relationship with Bob."

"Maybe she realizes that the less she says, the fewer lies she'll need to keep track of," Kyle contributed.

"Maybe, but if she doesn't start to cooperate, she's going to live out the rest of her life in prison."

"Don't worry; we'll figure this out," Tj assured her.

"Where do we even start?" Jenna sighed.

Good question. It would make things easier if there was a list of suspects with the means and motive to start with, but the way things had played out, the only way she was going to clear one friend was by proving another one guilty.

"If neither Bonnie nor Dennis killed our victim, then it was most likely someone else at the dinner," Tj asserted. "I suppose it's possible that someone else drove out to the resort and killed him, but with the snow and all, it seems unlikely. I guess we should start by trying to figure out if any of our other guests had a motive. I suppose everyone who was on the property that day had opportunity."

"This is crazy." Jenna sighed. "Even I have to agree that Dennis is the most likely suspect, but he says he didn't do it and I believe him. Bonnie insists she did, but I know she didn't. At the same time, I can't believe a single person at the dinner could have done something so horrible. Almost everyone present has been a close friend for most of my life. Maybe there was some serial killer lurking in the woods and Bob's death was random."

Tj just looked at Jenna.

"It could have played out that way," she defended herself.

"Really? A serial killer just happened to be lingering in the woods at the exact moment that a man pretty much everyone hated on sight decided to go for a walk?"

"Yeah, okay, I guess the theory is a long shot, but the only alternative is that someone I know and love killed a man in cold blood."

"What about Frannie's new guy?" Kyle asked. "He's probably the guest we know the least about. I think his first name is Arnie, but I don't think I ever caught his last name. I suppose I'm reaching, but his presence in our lives feels sudden and just a tad unconventional."

"It *is* an odd pairing," Tj agreed. "Frannie has never shown any interest in having a man in her life and, as far as I can remember, has never even dated; then all of a sudden she starts parading around town with some guy who's probably young enough to be her son. The whole thing is weird. Maybe this guy is up to no good and is using Frannie the way Bob used Bonnie. I guess I can try to have a chat with the guy."

"Yeah, but if we're wrong and start accusing this guy of any wrongdoing, it will really hurt Frannie," Kyle pointed out. "I'm sure she's sensitive about the fact that half of the town is gossiping about her new guy."

"Okay then, perhaps we should talk to Frannie," Jenna suggested.

"I'll do it tomorrow," Tj volunteered. "She has a couple of books on order for me, so I have an excuse to drop in. I'll do it at lunch."

"And I'll try to talk to Bonnie again," Jenna offered, "although I doubt it will do any good. She seems determined to be a martyr."

"I'm sure she feels responsible for all the trouble Bob's death has caused," Kyle said. "If she hadn't been fooled by the man, he would never have come to Paradise Lake and Dennis would never have been charged with murdering the SOB."

"Yeah, I guess you're right. I just wish we could wind back time and undo everything that's happened over the past week," Jenna said. "If Frannie's friend didn't do it, that means someone we know and love did. I'm not sure how any of us are supposed to live with that."

Chapter 8

Wednesday, December 3

"Can I have everyone's attention?" Tj yelled over the drone created by the eighteen members of the high-school ski team chatting among themselves. There was excitement spreading through the group as the fresh snow made for fantastic downhill conditions. Tj understood her students' excitement. There was nothing better than that first big snow of the season.

"As you all know, the town has voted to lengthen Christmas break from two weeks to three this year."

Everyone clapped and cheered.

"While this is wonderful news for most of you, I'm sure, it also means we have less time to prepare for the first of our regional meets, which is scheduled for the weekend after we return from break. Last year we dominated in regionals, and although a larger percentage than normal of last year's team graduated, I feel we have a real chance of winning again this year."

Tj paused as she calculated the number of school days between that moment and the beginning of the school holiday. She realized that, although the longer break from school would help her to juggle the other aspects of her life, including helping out at the resort, entertaining the girls, and investigating a murder, they were going to need to hustle if they were going to be ready for their first meet in January.

"We have a week and a half left to prepare, which, as I'm sure you all realize, isn't enough time to really be ready for what our competitors have to throw at us. While I won't require you to practice while on break, I'm going to strongly encourage you to do so. I'm sure there'll be plenty of snow on the slopes, so I want all of you out there as often as possible."

Everyone chanted that they would "ride, ride, ride."

Tj looked out the window of her classroom. There were huge flakes falling from a dark sky. Sometimes she wished she could leave all her responsibilities behind and spend her days on the slopes, as she knew many of her students did. Tj suspected that all the fresh powder would guarantee that most of her kids would spend most of their time on the mountain.

"I still need to select team captains. I usually appoint both a male and a female captain from the seniors, who have been with me the longest, and I have a couple of candidates in mind, but I'd like your input as well. I left sheets of paper on my desk. If you have someone you'd like to nominate, just leave me a note with the name of your candidate and the reason you think he or she would be a good captain. While it's tradition to choose seniors to fill these very important roles, there's no rule that the team captains must be seniors."

One of Tj's new team members, a sophomore with dark green eyes and deep red hair, raised her hand.

"You had a question?" Tj asked the petite athlete.

"Can you nominate yourself?"

Tj thought about it. "I suppose there's no rule against it; however, if you all nominate yourselves, we won't end up with anything other than a huge tie. Perhaps those of you who feel you should be team captain should make your case to your teammates, with the hope that one of them nominates you."

The girl turned and looked at the group. "As you all know, my name is Monica. I would be a good captain, so I think one of you should nominate me."

The girl sat down with a look on her face that seemed to convey that someone—probably one of the boys—would do as she asked.

One of the senior boys raised his hand. He wasn't a strong skier, but he was popular and could very well make a good team captain. "Instead of a boy and a girl, maybe you should choose a snowboarder and a skier. The events are so segregated these days. It's almost like two completely different sports."

"The idea has merit. What do you think?" Tj asked the class.

Pretty much everyone agreed.

"Okay; in other news, we'll meet at the bottom of Devil's Run at two o'clock this afternoon. Be dressed and ready to take to the hill. If any of you need a ride to the slopes, see me after class. We'll practice tomorrow as well but will take the weekend off, although, again, I encourage you all to head to the mountain as often as possible."

"You said we had the weekend off. What about Friday?" one of her new girls, a freshman with a ton of promise, asked.

"The tree lighting has been moved to Friday, so we won't be holding practice that day. I would encourage all of you to come out for the lighting ceremony. The school choir will be performing, and I'm certain they would appreciate your support."

"What time?" a freshman girl wearing a light pink sweater asked.

"The tree lighting is at five-thirty and the choir will perform until six. I believe there'll be a food vendor on site, and Santa will be holding court in the gazebo, if any of you have younger brothers and sisters."

"Is Angel Mountain planning to have their used ski swap like they did last year?" one of her returning students wondered.

"I believe so. While I haven't seen a list of the vendors who have signed up for booths this year, traditionally Angel Mountain has a presence. They usually have a representative selling season tickets, if any of your friends or family are in the market for a pass."

The downhill team members were all given free passes so they could practice whenever they wanted. As downhill coach, Tj received a free pass as well. This year she planned to purchase passes for Ashley and Gracie. She'd already been tearing up the slopes by the time she was their age.

"If there are no more questions, I'll leave you to work on your homework for the rest of the period," Tj wrapped up. "Remember, you must maintain a C or above in all your classes in order to be eligible for afterschool sports. I need you all, so *study*."

Luckily, most of her students cracked open their books and did just that. Tj decided to work on her own paperwork while her kids studied since she planned to use her lunch break to pay Frannie a visit at the library.

"Tj, how are you, dear?" Frannie greeted her when Tj walked into the library, one of her favorite places in town. Built as a bordello at the turn of the century, it had been converted into a library more than sixty years earlier, a few years after the town had been incorporated. The downstairs, which at one time had served as a common room for entertaining, held a large wooden counter that was now used as a reference desk but originally served as the bar on which the girls had danced to entertain the men.

"I'm doing fine. I came by to see if you had those books I requested."

"Actually, I do have them." Frannie placed three books on the counter. "I also have a book for Kallie. I know she's busy with holiday visitors and most likely won't make it in to pick it up. Would you mind taking it to her?"

"I'd be happy to."

Frannie turned to fetch Kallie's book and added it to Tj's pile.

"How are things going?" Frannie asked. "I haven't spoken to you since Thursday. I heard about what happened after I left." Frannie diverted her eyes and Tj frowned. There was no way Frannie would ever kill anyone, but she definitely looked like she was hiding something. Maybe Kyle wasn't so far off to suspect Arnie. Could Frannie be covering for him?

"It's been an interesting few days," Tj answered. She watched Frannie's expression as she continued. "I guess you heard Dennis was arrested for the murder of his mother's fiancé, but he was released when Bonnie herself confessed to the crime."

Frannie bent down as she stacked the books from the return bin onto the counter. "I had heard that. Surely no one believes Bonnie is guilty of such a serious crime?"

"I don't believe she did it, but it seems Sheriff Boggs is so happy to have the case wrapped up that he's pushing prosecution. Bonnie is out on bail now, but things are on track for trial at some point after the beginning of the year unless we can find the real killer. The problem is that all of our suspects are dear friends and neighbors, none of whom seem at all likely to kill a man. Kyle and I are doing what we can to help Bonnie. I know this is an awkward way to bring it up, but I wanted to know if you could tell me a bit more about your new boyfriend. Not that I'm accusing him of anything," Tj hurried to add.

Frannie looked up, surprise evident on her face. "You think Arnie might have killed Bonnie's fiancé?"

"No, it's not that." Tj tried to cover herself. "We're looking at everyone, but we're starting with the people who are new to the area and we know the least about."

"Arnie isn't new to the area. He's lived here quite a while, in fact," Frannie said. "He moved to Paradise Lake from Los Angeles a couple of years ago, after his wife died. I guess he came to visit a friend, fell in love with the area, and decided to stay."

"Maybe 'new to the area' isn't really accurate. It's more that he's new to our social circle. I mean, you only recently started spending time with him. Not that there's anything wrong with that. A lot of women enter into relationships with men who are significantly younger than they are."

Frannie laughed. "You think I'm a cougar? I suppose I should be flattered that you'd think me capable of such a feat, but the truth of the matter is, Arnie and I don't have a physical relationship. We're just people who have common interests and enjoy spending time together. When we first met he was still getting over his wife's death and wasn't really interested in a romance, and I'm not one to date, so we decided to become friends so we would both have someone to see a movie with, or attend social engagements together. "

"I'm so sorry." *Way to put your foot in your mouth, Tj.* "I just assumed."

"You know what they say about assuming." Frannie smiled. "I do understand why you might have gotten the wrong impression, though. Anyone who knows me knows that I don't spend time with men. Ever. I guess when Arnie and I started spending time together, it was natural for people to assume we were dating."

"So Arnie . . ." Tj continued, hoping Frannie would realize that she was inquiring about the likelihood that he had killed Bob King.

Frannie hesitated. "Arnie didn't kill Bob. He had no motive to do so. I, on the other hand, did have a motive. I'm only telling you this so I can also assure you that I didn't kill him."

Tj leaned on the table behind her. "You knew Bob King?"

"I not only knew him, I dated him. It was a long time ago and he was going by the name Rupert Kingston then."

"What happened?" Tj realized it was none of her business, but she found she couldn't keep herself from asking.

"I met Rupert in college. Although I wasn't looking for a relationship, he was a real charmer, and eventually I decided to take the plunge and give him my heart and body. We ended up living together for two wonderful years."

"And then?" Based on the fact that Frannie had never married, Tj suspected the answer to the question would be tragic and almost wished she hadn't asked.

"And then he graduated and I still had two years left until I received my degree. I loved him so much, and he'd told me many times that he loved me. I expected he'd wait for me to graduate so we could be married, but he didn't. After graduation he told me that he was going home to spend some time with his family but that he'd come back and we'd build a life together. I waited and waited and waited, but he never contacted me and he never came back. Eventually, I moved to Serenity and got on with my life."

"I'm so sorry."

Frannie looked directly at Tj. "I recognized Rupert the moment I arrived at the dinner. I felt so guilty and wasn't sure how to deal with the situation, so I pretended not to know him. I realized I needed to speak to Bonnie but decided it could wait until after Thanksgiving."

"I probably would have made the same decision, but why should you feel guilty?" Tj asked.

"I'm pretty sure the reason Rupert pursued Bonnie was because of me."

"You? Do you think he hooked up with her to make you jealous?"

Frannie shook her head. "No, I don't think it was that. It's just that Rupert came to Serenity over the summer. I was never so shocked in my life as when he walked in the library door. He claimed he'd been thinking about me and wanted to look me up. He said he missed me, that he had things to explain if I would give him the chance. I may be naive at times, but I wasn't born yesterday. It was evident to me that the only reason a man might come around after so many years is because he wanted something. I was polite but told him in no uncertain terms that I wasn't interested in renewing our friendship. He seemed really sad, so I took him to lunch at the Antiquery before I sent him on his way."

"And he met Bonnie?" Tj asked.

"He didn't meet her, but he noticed her. Bren was off that day, so Bonnie was covering for her on the floor while Jenna held down the fort in the kitchen. As always, she was friendly and cordial as she took our order. Other than a few pleasantries, we didn't speak, but Rupert asked me about her and I explained that she co-owned the restaurant and usually worked in the kitchen. I guess it came out that she was a widow. I really didn't think much about it until I saw Rupert at the dinner and realized that Bonnie's Bob and my Rupert were the same man. I assume he must have returned to the restaurant as Bob at some point after we shared our meal."

"So how did this Rupert, or Bob, or whatever his real name is, get Bonnie to attend that retreat?" Tj wondered.

"I don't know. You'll have to ask her. I will say that Rupert can be very charming and very persuasive. He has a knack for breaking down your defenses and making you trust him. He did it with me, and I can see how he would be successful with Bonnie. If I had to guess, he probably chose women who were inexperienced in the area of dating. He preyed on their desires to form intimate relationships while exploiting their corresponding fear of entering into them."

Tj sighed. Frannie was probably right. Bonnie had married early in life, so she never really had the chance to learn the cold, hard facts of the dating game. She'd had a happy marriage and Tj could understand that she might very well be nurturing the desire to replace what she'd lost, while at the same time be hanging on to her fear of doing so.

"I guess I will need to talk to Bonnie," Tj said.

"I think that would be a good idea, but I'd appreciate it if you didn't share my messy love story with anyone you don't absolutely have to. The whole thing is beyond embarrassing."

"Your secret is safe with me." Tj's heart bled for Frannie, but she realized that with Frannie's confession they were back to square one. If Arnie didn't kill Bob King, the killer probably was someone she knew and loved.

Chapter 9

Friday, December 5

It appeared the entire town had come out for the tree lighting. Mike had agreed to bring the family into town in the sleigh he used to provide a genuine backwoods experience for Maggie's Hideaway guests. Tj sat on the backseat with Jordan, Ashley, and Gracie, while, Mike, Ben, and Rosalie sat in the front. It really was a magical ride into town. Tj, Jordan, and the girls sang carols while light snow drifted down and covered their knit caps. As he always did when the family went for a sleigh ride, Ben made hot chocolate that he handed out in spill-proof cups after everyone was tucked in under a pile of blankets.

Once the family arrived, Mike tied up the horses well away from the loud noise created by the big crowd. Ashley followed Ben to where Jenna and Dennis were standing with their family, while Rosalie, Jordan, Gracie, and Tj squeezed in behind the people who were already there as best they could. Tj had attended the tree lighting ceremony every year of her life except for one. The year she had missed, she'd snuck away with Hunter for a quick kiss under the moonlight; in spite of their best intentions at the time, they never had made it back to see the giant tree light up the night sky.

"I've never ridden in a sleigh before," Jordan commented to Gracie, who was perched on his shoulders so she could see over the top of the crowd. "It was really fun. I especially liked the place where the tree branches grew over the trail like a canopy. You're lucky to live where you get so much snow."

"It doesn't snow on your boat?" Gracie asked. She had one red-mittened hand resting atop Jordan's head and the other resting comfortably on his shoulder.

"No, not usually," Jordan answered. Tj noticed the way he held on carefully to Gracie's feet, which were dangling across his chest.

"Does Santa come to your boat?" Gracie wondered as the town council began to gather around the tree for the official plugging in of the tree.

"No, I'm afraid he doesn't."

"How come?"

"Well," Tj smiled as Jordan struggled for an answer, "most of the time the boat I'm assigned to is very far out at sea."

"But Santa has a sleigh," Gracie reasoned. "He can fly to you and drop stuff off."

"True." Jordan was stuck, but Tj didn't feel inclined to help him out. "But our position in the ocean is usually secret, so Santa doesn't want to take the risk of being followed. You have to admit there are a lot of people watching out for him on Christmas Eve."

Gracie thought about that. "I saw a thing on TV last year where they were tracking Santa's trip. I guess it's a good thing he didn't come to your boat."

"Exactly. Santa knows that safety is the most important thing."

"Then it's good you're staying with us this year," Gracie decided. "He comes to the resort every year.

Last year he brought me a baby with blond hair, and this year he's bringing one with brown hair, like me. Ashley wants Santa to bring her a computer," Gracie continued. "What do you want him to bring you?"

Jordan looked surprised. "I don't know. I haven't thought about it. It's been a long time since I've celebrated Christmas."

"You don't even have Christmas on your boat?"

"Well, we have dinner, but we're usually working, so we don't exchange gifts or do much in the way of celebrating."

Gracie frowned. "Your mommy and daddy don't give you stuff?"

"My mom and dad passed away a long time ago, so it's just me."

Suddenly, Tj wanted to cry. Her first order of business next week was going to be to buy Jordan a stocking to hang on the fireplace and gifts to put inside.

"My mommy is dead too," Gracie informed Jordan. "And my daddy don't want me and Ashley, so we came to live with Tj."

Uh-oh. Tj noticed Jordan's frown at the daddy comment.

"It seems like it worked out okay," Jordan commented.

"Me and Ash like living with Tj, Papa, and Grandpa. Do you have a grandpa?"

"No, I'm afraid I don't."

"You should get one. Papa isn't our real grandpa, but Tj says he's like a real grandpa since he loves us so much. I bet if you asked someone you know who loved you a bunch like Papa loves us, they would want to be your grandpa."

Jordan squeezed Gracie's foot. Tj could tell that her innocent statement had really gotten to him. "Thanks for the tip. I'll think about it."

"Can we get more hot cocoa after the choir sings?" Gracie asked Tj.

"Yeah, that sounds good," Tj said.

"And can we go see Santa? I want to make sure he knows about my doll."

"Sure, baby, anything you want."

"Maybe you should ask Santa for something, since you aren't on your boat this year," Gracie suggested to Jordan. "You can come with me and Ashley."

Jordan smiled. "I don't really need much of anything."

"Christmas isn't about needing something; it's about *wanting* something," Gracie explained. "Tj got a snowboard last year even though she already had one."

Jordan looked at Tj.

"It's true," she replied.

"Oh look, they're starting." Gracie gasped as the choir began to sing and the huge fir tree as well as the gazebo lit up the night sky.

After the choir had finished their set, Mike and Rosalie went for coffee while Ben met up with his friends and Tj and Jordan took Ashley and Gracie to look at the decorated windows along Main Street. While all the windows contained imaginative displays, Tiz the Season, a store selling seasonal goods, tended to be the most extravagant year after year. This year the store's proprietor had outdone herself, with a fully functioning miniature ski resort all decorated for Christmas displayed in the window.

"Who knew so many people were in need of white lights and tree bulbs?" Jordan commented as they walked into the crowded store.

"'Tis the season," Tj said with a grin. "I want to look for some new decorations for the house. I'm not sure how we did it, but we somehow managed to use the house decorations in the resort lobby."

"Are we gonna get the tree this weekend?" Ashley asked.

"I'm hoping we can get it on Sunday, if the weather holds," Tj told her.

"Uncle Hunter wants to come with us so he can get one for his house," Ashley said.

"Where is Hunter?" Tj asked. "I saw him talking to you earlier, but he seems to have disappeared."

"His duck was quacking and then he left."

Jordan furrowed his brow. "His duck was quacking?"

"Uncle Hunter has a duck for a ring tone," Ashley explained. "He uses it to know when he's needed at the hospital. He's a doctor and has to go right away when they call him."

"I see."

"I was thinking that maybe we could decorate the tree using only red and purple decorations this year," Ashley suggested.

"But we have so many special ones I'd miss putting up," Tj countered.

"Then can I get my own tree for my room and decorate it however I want?"

"Sure. I think that would be a good idea. And we can get one for Gracie's room as well. How would you like to decorate your tree?" Tj asked.

"I don't want to look at decorations," Gracie whined. "Can't we go see Santa?"

Tj hesitated. She really did want to get the house decorated this weekend. Ever since Maggie's Hideaway had reopened they'd been slammed. If she didn't buy what she needed tonight, who knew when she'd get the opportunity?

"How about I help the girls get decorations for their little trees and then take them to see Santa?" Jordan offered. "You can do your shopping and we can meet in the ice cream shop for hot cocoa in, say, an hour?"

"Actually, that would be very helpful." Tj smiled. "If you get to the ice cream shop before me, just order me a coffee."

"The decorations I want are in the back," Ashley informed the adults.

"Okay, then let's get our own basket and check out those red and purple ornaments," Jordan said.

"I want baby animals on my tree," Gracie decided.

Tj watched as Ashley and Gracie hung on Jordan as he walked toward the aisle where the shopping baskets were located. In another circumstance she was sure he would have been a wonderful father to Gracie or anyone else. Tj could see how Jordan was exactly the type of guy her mom would go for, yet there was something nagging at her about the whole thing. Maybe she should have asked more questions about the night Gracie was conceived. At the time she and Hunter had interviewed Jordan, she was just so happy he wasn't planning to take Gracie from her that she hadn't wanted to rock the boat by grilling him.

"You here alone?" Kyle walked up and kissed Tj on the cheek.

"For the time being. Dad and Rosalie went for coffee, Grandpa took off with Bookman and Doc, Jenna and her family were exhausted so they headed home early, and Jordan took the girls to buy decorations for the little trees they're getting for their rooms and then to see Santa."

"I thought you were meeting Hunter."

"He had a duck emergency."

"Ah. My mom and Annabeth are looking at Christmas dresses, so I find myself at loose ends. Want to get a beer?"

"I'm on the prowl for Christmas decorations for the house, but I'd love to have some company while I shop."

Kyle shrugged and followed Tj down the aisle as she considered whether to get colored lights or white for the banister.

"So how are things going with Uncle Jordan?" Kyle asked. Although Tj and Kyle had seen each other almost every day between choir practice and play rehearsal, they hadn't had a chance to chat privately.

"Really good. He seems to be a genuinely nice guy who really wants nothing more than to get to know the daughter he never knew he had."

"But?" Kyle asked as Tj began loading white lights into her basket. "I can tell by your tone there's a *but*."

Tj sighed. "I'm not sure. I just have this nagging feeling that something doesn't add up."

"He seems to be who he says he is," Kyle confirmed. "I completed a pretty thorough background check before he arrived. He was born in Germany, grew up all over the world as the only child of a Navy family, went straight into the Naval Academy after graduating college, and has been working his way up the ladder ever since."

"Yeah, that all tracks, but there's something about the part where he's Gracie's biological father. The whole scenario feels off for some reason."

Tj began sorting through boughs of holly

"I confirmed that the man was in port on the night in question and that he was on the ship that set sail the following day," Kyle reminded her.

Tj frowned. She knew there was a problem with Jordan's story, but she couldn't put her finger on it. "Do you think these tall candles would look good on the mantel, or should I get these rounder, shorter ones?" she asked.

"I'd get the shorter ones," Kyle said. "They look sturdier, less likely to fall if they get bombarded by rolled-up socks like the mini fire catastrophe of last year."

"Good point."

The previous Christmas, Ashley and Gracie had been throwing sock balls at each other and had knocked a lit candle off the table, resulting in a small fire. Luckily, Tj had realized what had happened and put it out.

"You know," Tj continued as she moved on to the section with red and green bows in all shapes and sizes, "I think my trepidation has more to do with the actual meeting of my mom and Jordan. When Hunter and I interviewed him, he said he didn't even know my mom's last name. And it turned out she'd given him a fake first name too. He said they didn't talk about their lives. In the five years my mom was alive following that fateful night, she never once tried to contact the man she must have realized fathered her daughter. She dies in a car accident and a friend of hers, who I just realized I know nothing about, decides to contact Gracie's father after all of this time? Why?"

"Good question," Kyle admitted. "Maybe she felt that Jordan had the right to know he had fathered a child, but until your mom's death she'd been protecting her secret."

"Okay, then if we assume that last names and other personal information weren't exchanged between Jordan and my mom, how did this friend even know who he was or how to find him?"

Kyle picked up a piece from a nativity set on display and looked at the price tag stamped on the bottom. "Maybe after your mom found out she was pregnant she did some research and figured out who Gracie's father was, and for some reason she told the truth to this friend."

Tj thought about it. "If my mom knew who Gracie's father was and how to get hold of him, she would have hit him up for money. She was constantly in a state of financial crisis, and if she knew the identity of the man who fathered Gracie, I guarantee she would have looked at Jordan like he was a cash cow. The only reason she wouldn't hit the man up for money would be because she didn't know who he was."

"And if she didn't know who he was, she couldn't have told the friend," Kyle realized.

"Exactly. My mom slept around. Even if she realized the man she was married to wasn't the father of her baby, she probably had no way of figuring out which of the many men she had flings with was the father."

"If what you're saying is true, Jordan's story about the friend falls apart. Either he's lying about the whole thing or someone did send him a letter and that person is lying about what she knows and how she knows it."

"I'd like to find out more about this friend," Tj said.

Kyle tucked a large bear dressed in a Santa outfit under his arm. "I'll see what I can find out. I suppose you can start by asking Jordan if he's willing to share the identity of the woman who contacted him. I assume he checked her out before contacting an attorney."

"I'll ask him later. It's probably nothing, but I have this strange feeling that there's more going on than meets the eye."

Chapter 10

Sunday, December 7

By Sunday afternoon the weekend visitors had checked out, bringing a brief lull to the busy resort. Tj packed a basket with sandwiches and hot cocoa while Mike tracked down the ax they would need to cut down the Christmas trees they would require. The family always displayed a fifteen-foot tree in the living room, but in addition to the tree that would grace the main part of the house and the small trees the girls wanted for their rooms, Ben usually looked for a medium-size tree for his bedroom suite and Tj cut a tall, slim tree for her room.

Doc, Bookman, Hunter, and Kyle and his family, decided to come along to pick out trees for their residences, and while the staff from the resort would cut a six-foot tree for each cabin, Mike usually liked to pick out the tree for the lobby himself. Given the large number of trees that would be required, and the many friends and family members who'd asked to go along, Mike hooked up three sleighs, each pulled by two horses. Mike drove the sleigh that carried Rosalie, Ben, Doc, and Bookman, while Kyle drove the one that carried his dog Trooper, his mom Vicki, Annabeth, Jordan, Ashley and Gracie, and Tj, Echo, and Hunter followed behind in the open sleigh that they'd use to transport the trees.

"The resort looks great," Hunter commented as the caravan of horse-drawn sleighs started down the snow-packed trail.

Tj nodded. "The staff did an excellent job."

In addition to stringing white lights in the fir trees surrounding the lodge, the staff had hung colored lights along the eaves of the lodge, the restaurant, and all twenty cabins. During the summer the resort was filled with people who booked space in the campground, but during the winter the guests were limited to the twenty cabins, as well as the hotel rooms located on the second story of the lodge. While the resort would be booked to capacity when it got a bit closer to the holiday, with the campground closed, the restaurant and bar tended to be much less crowded than it was during the busier summer months.

The resort's activities director had turned the lobby of the lodge, as well as the activities center, into a magical wonderland with lights, evergreen boughs, and mechanical displays that fascinated the children who spent their holiday at Paradise Lake. Mike had always treated his guests like family, and over the years the resort had acquired several groups who returned every year to spend the holidays with the Jensens. One of the best things about the arrangement was that Tj had developed relationships with some of the guests, who seemed to replace the aunts, uncles, and cousins she'd never had growing up.

"The Cartwrights are coming for Christmas this year," Tj informed Hunter, referring to a family with a grandfather, great-aunt, mom, dad, and three children—two boys and a girl—who were about the same age as Hunter and Tj. When they were all younger, the Cartwright children had spent many a summer evening at the beach with Hunter and Tj. As the offspring grew up, they began skipping the family outing, so it had been a few years since Tj had seen anyone from the younger generation.

"Are Conrad and his wife coming?" Hunter wondered. Conrad was the eldest son, who had recently gotten married to a girl neither Hunter nor Tj had met yet.

"They are, and Dad said April and her husband are bringing Kyla, the baby. I can't wait to meet her." April was the only daughter, and the middle child. During their teen years April had had a huge crush on Hunter, following him around whenever she got the opportunity.

"It seems so odd that April is married with a baby," Hunter said. "I know it's been a few years, but it seems like yesterday she was following me around, trying to show off her new smile after she got her braces off."

"Does this mean we're getting old?" Tj asked. "I always figured when I started making statements that began with 'seems like yesterday,' that would be a sign that I was getting old."

Hunter laughed. "Yeah, I guess maybe we are getting on in years. Won't be all that long until we're sitting on the porch, talking about the good old days when we had the energy to go out and cut our own tree rather than buying one from the lot in town."

"Do you think we'll still be friends when we're old enough to buy a tree from the lot?" Tj asked.

"I hope so." Hunter smiled and held her hand in spite of the fact that they both had gloves on.

Lost in their own thoughts, they sat quietly as the trail paralleled the water. The lake had many moods and at times bore waves rivaling the ocean, but today the air was calm and overcast, with just a few snow flurries dancing through the air, and the surface of the water was so calm it reflected the surrounding mountains like a sheet of glass.

"I'm sorry Jake decided not to come," Tj said as the sleighs turned toward the forest and slowly began their climb to the top of the rise, where the best trees could be found.

"His joints have been bothering him and he didn't think he could take spending so much time in the cold. He'll help me to decorate when I get home."

After Jake had suffered a heart attack, Hunter had insisted that his grandfather move in with him so he could keep an eye on him. His sister Chelsea had moved into the house as well after a bad breakup, but she was still on the East Coast with her parents and would be until after the New Year.

"Did you ever ask Jordan about the letter he received?" Hunter asked.

After her conversation with Kyle the previous Friday, Tj had called Hunter to fill him in on their discussion.

"I did. He said the letter was simply signed *A*. He was unable to track the letter to its source, but the details provided were accurate, and when he saw a photo of Gracie, he realized the woman most likely knew what she was talking about."

"While I agree that Jordan and Gracie bear a resemblance to each other, there are a lot of people with similar features who aren't related," Hunter pointed out. "Maybe we really should do genetic testing just to be sure."

"Yeah, maybe." Tj glanced at the sleigh in front of them, where Jordan was sitting on the backseat with Ashley and Gracie. They were all laughing about whatever it was they were talking about. Whether Jordan and Gracie were related or not, he did seem to fit in with the family, and he didn't have anyone of his own. He wasn't asking for anything, so Tj still wasn't inclined to rock the boat. "Is there a way we can do the testing without Jordan knowing about it?" Tj asked.

"I suppose there are ways to get the samples you need without revealing your intention, but I wouldn't recommend going that route. Jordan has been straight with us, so I think we should be straight with him."

"You're right. I guess I need some time to think about it."

Hunter shrugged. "If you decide you want to pursue testing let me know and I'll take care of the details. By the way, I received the official autopsy report for Bob King. It turns out the cause of death was a blow to the side of the head. He also had a black eye, which would indicate that he fought with his killer."

"So Bonnie is off the hook," Tj realized. "She would never try to duke it out with a man."

"Not entirely. Bonnie confessed to killing him in a fit of rage, and Boggs is buying it for now."

"That's ridiculous."

"Maybe, but Boggs wants to believe Bonnie is guilty because it's easier, and I doubt Bonnie will back off on her confession until she's sure Dennis is in the clear."

Tj laid her head on Hunter's shoulder as she tried to figure out what to do next. The answer didn't appear to be an easy one, and she didn't want thoughts of the man to mar the perfection of the afternoon, so she closed her eyes and tried to think happier thoughts. Being with Hunter again for the holidays had brought back so many wonderful memories. They'd been so close before the breakup. When they'd been in high school they'd been inseparable, and during the first years in college they'd spent every minute together during their trips home during school breaks.

And then, Tj remembered, Hunter had given in to pressure from his mom and her fairy tale had ended.

"Something on your mind?" Hunter asked.

"I was thinking of the first time we went tree cutting together. We had just started dating and I invited you to go with us. You made some comment about your mom ordering your tree from a decorator and it really hit me how different our upbringings were, Maybe I should have realized right then that things between us would never work out."

"What makes you think they'll never work out?" Hunter asked.

Tj just looked at him.

"Okay, I'll admit we hit a bump, but that doesn't mean we can't still have our happily ever after. We do seem to be drawn to each other, and we have a lot of wonderful memories to build on."

Tj smiled. "Like when we were freshmen in college. We both came home about this time of year and went tree cutting together, just the two of us."

Hunter grinned. "That has to be one of my favorite memories. I still have that blanket. I keep it on the foot of my bed."

Tj blushed, remembering what they had done on the blanket. "I'm glad you decided to come with us this year. It's been a long time since we've done this together."

"Maybe this will mark the restart of an annual tradition," Hunter said.

Tj lifted her head from his shoulder and looked at his profile. "However things work out, I really do hope we continue to be in each other's lives until we end up in those rockers on the porch."

Hunter smiled. "Yeah, me too. Right now, how about we team up to find a tree Jake will love?"

"You got it." Tj called Echo, who jumped down out of the sleigh. She walked over to where the others were unloading. "Ash, Gracie, do you want to come with Uncle Hunter and me to find the trees for your room?"

"I want Uncle Jordan to help me," Gracie responded.

Tj tried not to be hurt that Gracie didn't want to team up with her, but even she had to admit that Jordan had been doting on the girls while she had been busier than usual lately.

"How about we all look around together?" Jordan offered.

Tj shrugged. "Yeah, okay. There are some nice white firs up on the hill." She turned to look at Hunter. "Grab an ax."

Hunter picked out an ax while Tj and Jordan made sure the girls were bundled up warmly for their trek through the snow.

"Do you do this every year?" Jordan asked once they'd started their hike.

"Every year," Tj confirmed.

"Are these trees really all that much better than the ones for sale in town?"

"Not at all; the tree lot in Serenity has a crew that cuts fresh trees they sell within a few days. But hiking up the mountain, finding the perfect tree, carting it down the hill to the sleighs while trying to regain the feeling in your fingers and toes is all part of the fun. Tree cutting isn't about getting a tree as much as it is about creating a memory."

Jordan smiled. "I like that. It's been so long since I've even had a tree. This will be a nice memory to take with me when I leave."

After the small group had selected a huge tree for Hunter's house and small ones for each of the girls' rooms, they decided to carry what they had back down the hill and check in with the others. Mike had been successful in finding a tree for the lobby, but Doc, Bookman, and Ben were still looking. Rosalie gave the girls hot cocoa while Hunter and Jordan loaded the trees.

"Aren't you getting a tree for your room?" Ashley asked Tj.

"If we have time I might look around a bit."

"Can Uncle Jordan watch me and Gracie so we can sled down that hill over there? I really don't want to hike on the hill anymore."

Tj glanced at Jordan.

"Fine by me," he said.

"You want to come help me?" Tj turned to Hunter.

"I'd be delighted."

Tj, Hunter, and Echo set back up the hill. This time they headed toward a different grove of trees.

"I can't feel my toes, but this is fun," Hunter commented. "And Echo seems to be having a good time."

Tj watched her dog as he chased a squirrel up a tree. "He loves to have the chance to spend the day in the snow. He gets hot with all that thick black fur."

"Are you looking for a tall tree?" Hunter asked.

"Tall and slim. I think a silver tip would work well. I have a high ceiling in my room, but there's so much furniture in there, I don't have enough floor space for a tree that's wide and bushy."

"It looks like we aren't the only ones with the idea of searching this particular grove." Hunter nodded toward a set of footprints in the snow.

"Footprints." Tj gasped as she experienced a feeling of déjà vu. "Of course; why haven't I thought of that before?"

"I feel like I missed the preview." Hunter stopped walking and looked at her.

"There were footprints in the snow when I tripped over Bob King's body. A single set that had already been covered by snow to a degree but were still discernible."

"And . . . ?" Hunter prompted.

"They were huge. There's no way they belonged to Bonnie."

"But they could have belonged to Dennis," Hunter reminded her.

"Yeah, that's true. I seem to remember a waffle-type pattern that's most often found in men's work or hiking boots. Part of me thinks I should call Roy and tell him what I remembered, but another part doesn't want to be responsible for landing Dennis back in jail so close to Christmas. The sheriff doesn't *really* believe Bonnie did it, so he's fine allowing her to be out on bail, but Dennis might be another story altogether."

"I guess if he asks . . ." Hunter left the thought unfinished.

"Yeah, if he asks I'll tell him; otherwise I'll leave it alone for now. Although . . ."

"Although?" Hunter prompted.

Tj closed her eyes as she tried to picture the scene the night she found Bob King buried in the snow. "There was only one set of footprints," she realized. "Bob must have been killed somewhere else and then carried to the spot where I tripped over him."

"Why would someone go to all the trouble of moving the body?" Hunter asked.

"I don't know, but I have a feeling the answer to that question could point us to the killer."

Later that evening, after the all the trees had been decorated, the pizza consumed, the baths given, and the sisters tucked into bed, Tj sat alone in front of the crackling fire. It wasn't really all that late, but everyone was tired, so Jordan had retired to his cabin and her dad and grandfather had gone to their respective rooms. Cuervo was curled up in Tj's lap, purring loudly as she scratched him behind the ears and Echo was snoring from his bed near the fire.

The tree really did look beautiful. Fifteen feet of colored lights accentuated hundreds of colorful bulbs and handcrafted ornaments that had been collected by the Jensen family since before she was born. Every year Tj was treated to a walk down memory lane as she hung the special pieces that had belonged to her grandmother and other loved ones no longer with them, and every year Tj argued with her dad that they really didn't need to hang every lopsided ornament she'd made for him when she was a child.

Now Tj had Ashley and Gracie to contribute their own handmade pieces to the collection. Jordan had decided to decorate the tree in his cabin, and Ashley and Gracie had both pitched in to create dough ornaments, paper chains, and hand-painted ornaments. Tj could see how touched he was by their efforts. She thought about Hunter's offer to have the paternity test done. It would answer once and for all whether Jordan was actually Gracie's father, but as she watched him with the girls, she asked herself if it really mattered.

Tj took a sip of her wine as she thought about the future. She wondered how things would progress if Jordan really was Gracie's biological father. Would he change his mind about wanting custody of the child he had every right to, or would he continue to honor his promise to leave things as they were? What about when Gracie got older; did they owe it to her to tell her the truth? And how would that affect both Gracie and Ashley?

Echo must have sensed her distress because he got up from his napping place and wandered over to the couch. He sat down in front of her and placed a paw on her lap. Tj smiled at the big dog who always seemed to know when she was in need of comfort.

"So what should I do?" Tj asked the dog, who tilted his head as he appeared to be trying to understand.

Echo leaned forward and placed his head in Tj's lap, much to Cuervo's annoyance. Tj scratched him behind the ears as she tried to figure out the next move in her continuously complicated life. The more she thought about it, the more certain she was that tracking down the faceless *A* who had sent Jordan the letter was an important thing to do. Jordan had no way of knowing how vastly unlikely it was that her mother had known his real name.

On the other hand, as much as it made no sense to her that her mother had known who Jordan was and not hit him up for money, it also made no sense that some random person would figure everything out and then inform Jordan of his probable state of parenthood after all this time.

Maybe someone who knew both Jordan and her mom had seen them together in the bar, and after Gracie was born this unidentified person had realized that she must belong to him. But who would have seen them who would have known who both of them were? The bartender? Another patron? Tj was willing to bet that her mom frequented the bar fairly regularly, and if Jordan was leaving from port the next morning, it made sense that the bar was near the port.

Of course, after her mother divorced the man she'd been married to when Gracie was conceived she'd moved from the area, so if the person in the know was someone like the bartender, they most likely wouldn't have kept in touch.

There was one thing for sure: the mystery behind the letter seemed to become more and more complicated as she considered the possible explanations.

"Ready for bed?" she asked Echo.

He thumped his tail without lifting his head.

Cuervo yawned and stretched out his front legs when Tj pushed him off her lap. He gave her a dirty look for disturbing him as she got up from the sofa to begin turning off the lights. Tj supposed that however Jordan came into her life, she was grateful for his presence. He'd been a huge help with the girls, and he seemed to have a calming effect on both Helen and Bonnie as well. Maybe one day he would leave the sea behind and settle down with a family of his own.

Chapter 11

Wednesday, December 10

"My mom called," Nikki informed Tj later that week. The two were sitting together in the Serenity High School teachers' lounge during lunch. "She really wants me to come home over Christmas break. At first I was so depressed about Carl leaving that I didn't think I could deal with all of my happily married siblings and their two-point-five perfect children, but then I realized that hanging out with my family will be a lot better than sitting home alone."

"It'll be good for you to spend the holidays with your family," Tj agreed. "You're always saying what a good cook your mom is, and how much you miss your family's annual traditions when you don't make it home."

"That's true, but my oldest sister just had a baby and my middle sister just found out she's pregnant with her second child. And to make matters worse, my brother and his wife have decided to adopt and my baby sister just got engaged. Everyone will be celebrating something except me. I'll end up feeling like the spinster aunt with too many cats."

"You don't have any cats and you're way too young to be a spinster," Tj pointed out. "There may be a few difficult moments in the beginning, but over all I think you'll have a fabulous time. And if they get to be too much, you can always check into a motel."

Nikki laughed. "I might have to do that. Mom is already into full matchmaker mode. She suggested that I look up some of my old boyfriends. Like I want to go out with anyone I went to high school with."

"You seem to be pushing me to formalize my relationship with Hunter and he was my high-school boyfriend," Tj reminded her.

"That's different. Hunter is really great. Any girl would be lucky to have him, and if you don't snatch him up, someone else is going to."

"And the guys you dated in high school weren't great?" Tj asked.

Nikki thought about it. "There was this one guy. He was a jock and a good student, and he wasn't as stuck up as his teammates. Everyone called him Joeystein."

"'Cause he was a Frankenstein-type monster?"

"No, the name was an amalgam of Joe Montana and Einstein because he was so good in math *and* he was the captain of the football team. Also his name was Joe."

"And you dated this well-rounded guy?"

"For a while. We seemed to end up pitted against each other in quite a few academic contests that created a rivalry that led to a huge argument. We didn't have the maturity to realize that the fight was stupid and let it break us up."

"So is this Joeystein going to be home for the holidays as well?" Tj asked.

"I really don't know."

"If he is, you should give him a call. Have coffee. Catch up on old times."

"He could be married," Nikki said.

"True," Tj acknowledged. "Okay, if he isn't married or in any type of romantic relationship, you should take him out for a spin if you have the opportunity. Life is short."

Nikki appeared to be thinking about it. She had a dreamy look on her face as she nibbled on her tuna sandwich, which Tj was certain was directly due to thoughts of Joeystein.

"Speaking of life being short, I may have a clue for you in the axed fiancé case."

Tj looked up from her own lunch. "What kind of clue?"

"I had a conversation with the manager of the Serenity Motor Inn the other day. His son is flunking math, and I wanted to make sure he had the names of a couple of good tutors. Anyway, we got to chatting and he mentioned that he had seen a photo of Bob King in the paper and swears that a man who looked exactly like him checked into one of his rooms under another name last summer."

Tj realized that Rupert Kingston must have stayed at the Motor Inn when he was in town trying to court Frannie. "Did he say anything about what name he used or why he was here?"

Nikki scrunched her brow as she thought about it. "I think he mentioned a name, but I'm not sure I can remember it. He also said that the man had a parade of women coming and going from his room while he was there."

"Did he mention who these women were?"

"No, and I didn't ask. You can go out there and talk to him directly if you want. I suppose if this guy was Bob King using a different name, the fact that he was in town prior to this visit could be huge."

"How so?" Tj asked.

"It increases the size of your suspect pool considerably," Nikki pointed out. "If he was in town, and if during his visit he engaged in intimate activities with several women, there has to be a jealous husband, boyfriend, or outraged brother or father in the mix somewhere. Not to mention the women themselves. Chances are he charmed them the same way he did Bonnie and then left them without another thought when his business was done."

Tj thought about it. Nikki was right. She knew that Rupert Kingston had been in town the previous summer, and that he was the same man who had shown up as Bob King because Frannie had told her so. If the man was in town for several days and he had been dipping his pole into the pond made up of the town's female population, he must have made *someone* mad. Was it possible that that someone came out to the resort and killed the man while all of the invited guests were inside?

Later that evening, Tj was sitting at a table in the lobby when Kallie walked in. It was after dinner and the lodge was quiet. Normally, Tj didn't work at the resort on the days she taught, but the desk clerk had called in sick so she'd volunteered to cover the phones until closing. Working on quiet evenings really wasn't bad because she was able to catch up on the mountain of paperwork that always seemed to be cluttering her desk while her grandpa saw to the girls. On this particular evening a light snow was falling outside the huge picture window that looked out onto the lake. The staff had set up a Santa and twelve reindeer covered in white lights on the lawn outside the window. The scene, combined with the Christmas jazz playing on the stereo, was truly magical.

"Tj, can I talk to you?" Kallie asked.

"Sure. Have a seat." Tj pointed toward a chair. "What can I do for you?"

Kallie stood nervously in front of her. She twisted a piece of paper in her hands, which Tj figured would be illegible once she got to the point of her visit. "I know you don't usually allow your employees to take vacation days during the Christmas rush, but I need to ask if you can make an exception in my case. I really need next week off." Kallie paused. She shoved the time-off request toward Tj. "It's important or I wouldn't ask."

Tj frowned. Kallie was new as the restaurant manager. It wasn't going to go over well with anyone if Tj allowed her to take time off during the holiday. One of the main reasons they closed in November was so employees could spend time with their families before the Christmas rush. If she let Kallie go during one of the busiest times of the year and not the other employees, who she knew would like time off if given the chance, it would be bad for morale.

"When we hired you, we informed you about our no-vacation-over-Christmas policy and you said you were fine with that," Tj reminded her.

"I know. But I thought I would be able to visit," Kallie paused, "my family over Thanksgiving. As you know, it didn't work out."

"Maybe we can work something out after New Year's," Tj said.

"No!" Kallie took a deep breath. "It has to be next week."

Tj hesitated, uncertain how to proceed. Kallie was good in the restaurant and she hated to lose her, but not only was she a manager—and therefore supposed to set an example for the rest of the staff—but she was their newest full-time employee as well.

"Maybe you should tell me exactly why it's so important for you to have next week off."

Kallie took another deep breath before she spoke. "I have a son. He's four. I love him so very, very, much." A tear slid down Kallie's cheek. "Two years ago my husband died."

"Oh, Kallie, I'm so sorry," Tj sympathized. "I had no idea."

"Silent Night" played in the background as Kallie gathered her thoughts. "I don't like to talk about it and you never directly asked me about it during my interview, so I didn't bring it up."

Kallie looked up at the ceiling as she struggled with fresh tears. "Anyway," she continued, "after Alton died I had a hard time making ends meet. My husband was from a wealthy family and his parents never approved of our relationship, so they cut him off when he refused to stop seeing me. At the time it didn't seem to matter. We were in love and able to make our own way. And then I got pregnant with Brady. I had a tough pregnancy and was unable to work. We managed to get by, but just barely. During the time I was off work we burned through the small savings we had."

Tj waited for Kallie to go on.

"After Brady was born my husband and I talked about the fact that I really needed to go back to work, but child care was so expensive. I got a job waiting tables in the evening and Alton worked days, so there was really only a short period of time between when I had to leave for work and Alton got home. After a *lot* of discussion we decided to talk to Alton's mother about paying for child care for Brady. He was, after all, her only grandchild, and she had plenty of money. At first she refused, but when Brady was almost two she agreed to allow him to stay at her house a few hours a day while I was at work."

"And Alton's dad?" Tj asked.

"He isn't really in the picture. I mean, the couple are still married and live in the same house and make a point of being seen in public together, but everyone knows he has his women and she has her charities. Alton's dad travels a lot, so it's really his mom who runs the house and makes family decisions."

"Wow. That seems like a lonely way to live."

"It is. I tried to establish a relationship with my mother-in-law, but she made it clear she wasn't interested. After Alton's death everything got worse between us. I didn't know how to deal with her grief and unreasonable behavior when my own world had fallen apart. I knew I had to get a full-time job just to feed us. Surprisingly, Alton's mom agreed to keep Brady the extra hours."

"She probably found comfort in his presence," Tj supposed.

"I guess. She still wanted nothing to do with me, but she seemed to enjoy spending time with my son. After I had been at my job for six months, my new boss hit on me. I made it clear I wasn't interested in anything other than a professional relationship, but the man wouldn't take no for an answer. When I threatened to file a sexual harassment suit, he fired me. To make a long story short, I was unable to get another job right away, and since I had no savings to bridge the gap, I lost my apartment. Alton's parents agreed to allow Brady to live with them but not me. I knew as long as I was homeless, living with his grandparents was the best thing for my baby, so I allowed him to stay with them. The problem was that after a while they convinced themselves that I was an unfit mother and sued for custody."

"Oh, Kallie, I'm so sorry." Tj leaned forward and wrapped her hand around the young mother's. "Did the court side with them?"

"They did. They got my former scumbag of a boss to testify that he fired me because I stole from him. He lied and said I'd come on to *him* and when he turned me down I went into a rage and destroyed his property. I did nothing of the kind, but it was the word of a businessman versus a homeless, unemployed ex-waitress. The judge believed my in-laws and my ex-boss and my baby was taken away from me."

Tj suddenly wanted to strangle this nameless ex-boss.

"I have scheduled visitation and that's all," Kallie said before Tj could ask about the lowlife who had ruined Kallie's life. "I was supposed to spend Thanksgiving week with my boy, but my former in-laws decided to go to Aspen and took Brady with them. I just heard from them, and they offered me next week or nothing at all. I need this job, Tj. Having a steady job is the only way I'm ever going to be able to convince the court that I'm competent and should have my son back. And it's been so long since I've seen Brady. I'll just die if I can't hold my baby in my arms."

Tj gathered her thoughts. She felt bad for the poor woman and wanted to help her, but she knew giving her a week off during their busiest time was going to make her unpopular with the rest of the staff. She could explain the situation to the other managers, and that might buy Kallie some sympathy, but the hourly employees who worked under her were never going to respect her if she wasn't down in the trenches with them when it was crunch time.

"I'll need to run this past my dad. Our policy is very strict for a reason, but given the circumstances, I'm sure we can work something out. Would you be able to bring Brady here to the resort?" Tj asked.

Kallie hesitated. "I'm not sure. Maybe. I usually just get a hotel room near my in-laws' house. I can't afford much, but it's convenient, and I don't have anywhere else to go."

Tj really wanted to help the young mom, but she also didn't want to agree to a situation that would make Kallie ineffective as a manager. "Off the top of my head, I can say without hesitation that if you're able to bring Brady to the resort, we can set you both up in one of the guest rooms in the lodge. I'd offer you a cabin, but they're all booked for the entire week. When you're at work, either I or one of my family can keep an eye on your little guy for you. That way you can have your visit and not miss work."

"You would do that for us?" Kallie started to cry. "That is so nice."

"I understand how much a child can mean to you and am happy to help. Talk to your in-laws and let me know if that works out for you."

Kallie got up and hugged Tj. "Thank you. I'll call them right now."

Chapter 12

Friday, December 12

Tj drove through the town of Serenity on her way to pick up Ashley and Gracie from the Antiquery. She had been at Angel Mountain Ski Resort, holding the last official downhill practice until after the holiday break. The girls had had play rehearsal after school, so Jenna had volunteered to take them back to the restaurant and have Tj pick them up there. Tj knew Jenna was busy baking cookies for the annual cookie exchange, which would be held at Helen's house the following evening.

Now that school was out for the holiday, it was beginning to really feel like Christmas. Tj listened to a radio station that played nonstop Christmas music as she slowly made her way along Main Street. The entire town was ablaze with colorful lights, creating the feel of a Christmas card. Flurries were drifting through the air, adding to the holiday atmosphere while not really impacting either the roads or the throngs of shoppers who were strolling among the festively decorated shops. Tj pulled off the main drag and into the alley behind the popular antique store and restaurant. She parked her car next to Jenna's, then made her way up the short flight of stairs and into the back door, which opened directly into the kitchen.

"Something smells good," Tj commented as she removed her hat, gloves, and scarf. She hung them, along with her heavy down ski jacket, on a hook in the back storage room.

"I'm trying out a new cookie for the exchange," Jenna said. "Try one."

Tj picked up one of the still warm cookies. It was soft, with a chewy texture and an interesting flavor that made her think of hot chocolate in front of a fire after a day of building a snowman. "This is really good. It tastes just like hot cocoa; the good kind made with heavy cream."

"Good." Jenna smiled. "That's what I was going for. What kind of cookie are you bringing to the exchange this year?"

"Oreos?"

"The cookies are supposed to be homemade," Jenna pointed out.

"I know, but I've been so busy that I haven't had a chance to come up with anything. I was going to have Grandpa make something for me, but he's been helping Dad check in the new arrivals, so I hated to ask. The resort is going to be bursting at the seams for the next three weeks."

"Why don't you ask Kallie to make you some cookies? She's a really good cook, and I'm sure she'd make you something wonderful to bring."

Tj took another bite of her cookie and then headed toward the walk-in refrigerator for a pitcher of milk. She'd never gotten a chance to have lunch and was starving. "Kallie had to take her days off to go pick up her son."

"I didn't even know she had a son," Jenna said as she slipped two cookie sheets into the oven. "In fact, I didn't even know she was married."

"She's not." Tj poured cold milk into a tall glass. "At least not anymore. It's a long story." Tj explained what had occurred and then added, "Her week with Brady starts on Sunday, so I let her leave early today and take tomorrow and Sunday off as her regular days so that she could drive to LA and pick him up. Both she and her son are going to stay with us for the week so that she can have her visit *and* work."

Jenna slid the cookies that had been cooling off from a cookie sheet and onto a plate. "Wow, that's really terrible. I can't imagine losing one of my children. Is she trying to regain custody?"

"She said she was, but that she has to prove she can hold a job and maintain a stable environment. She works at the resort but lives in one of those little studios down by the river. I'm going to talk to Dad about helping her out with a nicer apartment. I can't see a judge being thrilled with her current living arrangements since the in-laws are loaded and able to provide a mansion for the boy to live in."

Jenna looked shocked. "The in-laws are loaded and they aren't helping her out?"

Tj finished her milk and set her glass in the sink. "I got the impression that the in-laws wanted custody of their grandson and were willing to do whatever it took to make that happen. Kallie indicated that her ex-boss fired her because she wouldn't sleep with him and then turned it around during the custody hearing to make it sound as if she came on to him so he had to let her go. The whole thing sounds like one big mess, if you ask me."

"Apricot amaretto or oatmeal crisp?" Jenna asked.
"Huh?" Tj asked.

"Which kind of cookie do you want to bring to the cookie exchange?"

"Oh, the oatmeal. Do you have all the ingredients?"

"I do."

"Thanks; I really appreciate it." Tj looked at the clock on the wall. "I probably should get going. I have a ton of things to do once I get home. Are Ashley and Gracie up front?"

"Yeah. They're helping Mom in the shop."

"I'm anxious to see what your mom did with the display she's been working on."

"Her theme is Christmas in the twenties. She has all sorts of antique decorations she found at an estate sale over the summer. She used some of the period pieces she had in the antique store to create a living room setting. It's really pretty awesome. There's even a glass Santa-and-reindeer set that was my great-grandmother's. Mom usually displays it on the dining table in her house, but she decided to bring it here this year since it went so well in the display."

"Isn't she afraid it will get broken?" Tj asked.

"She says she's not, but personally, I wish she'd left the heirloom at home."

"My grandma left behind a box of ornaments she had as a child," Tj said. "Grandpa is always really careful about where they're displayed. There are some things that just can't be replaced."

Jenna removed another batch of cookies from the oven using her Mr. and Mrs. Claus oven mitts. Paired with her Santa's workshop apron, Jenna looked like Mrs. Claus herself, although Mrs. Claus was usually pictured as short and heavy, with short graying hair, and Jenna was tall and slim, with long blond hair that brushed her waist when it wasn't confined to a braid or hairnet.

"Bonnie has a box of stuff from Dennis's grandmother that she displays every year, but this year she hasn't done a single thing to decorate her house," Jenna added. "I guess I can see why she's so distracted, but it seems like such a shame that she's missing the holiday. I hope we can find the real killer and get this wrapped up in time for the entire Elston family to pull a little joy from the season."

Tj felt bad for Jenna. With both Dennis and Bonnie under Sheriff Boggs's microscope, it was going to be hard for the family to fully embrace the joy of the holiday. Tj knew that Jenna was doing everything in her power to create a sense of normalcy but, truth be told, there were only so many cookies you could bake or decorations you could display.

"Kallie lost custody of her child?" Kyle asked later that evening. Tj and he were playing cards with Ben, Doc, and Bookman. The girls were in bed and Mike was out with Rosalie.

"Yup," Tj confirmed as she discarded an unwanted eight. "Her boss came on to her and when she said no, she was fired. She lost her job *and* her apartment. The mother-in-law sued for custody, claiming Kallie was an unfit mother, and won."

"Do you think it's possible the in-laws were in on it the entire time?" Bookman asked.

Tj frowned. "What do you mean?"

"Consider the sequence of events," Bookman suggested after discarding a seven. "Based on what you've shared, it sounds as if the husband's parents are really only in the marriage for appearances. It sounds like the wife is home alone quite often, while her husband is away on business or courting other women. Her only child dies, leaving a hole in her life. I realize the woman had been estranged from the son, but I would be willing to bet that the estrangement was a direct result of a father wanting to control his offspring, rather than a mother not wanting a relationship with her son. Anyway, the mother-in-law is living with this huge void and she realizes she has a grandson who, I'm guessing, reminds her of her son when he was young. There's a good chance her role as a mother was the only thing that really gave her life purpose, so she latches on to her grandchild and manipulates things so that she can have him as an everyday part of her life."

"The woman does sound like a cold witch," Tj said. "It's hard for me to see her as a sympathetic character."

"Most cold witches have a reason for being heartless," Bookman proposed. "It's hard to understand why the woman made the choices she did. She most likely blames Kallie for the loss of her son from her life, and it's possible the woman might even blame Kallie for her son's death in some twisted way. She realizes she wants to establish a relationship with the grandson now that her son is gone, but she still wants nothing to do with the woman her son left her for."

"'Left her'?" Ben asked. "That makes it sound like Kallie is the other woman rather than her son's wife."

"Mother and son relationships can be complex," Bookman explained. "In order to understand why a person might act in a certain manner, you really need to know their story. My guess is that no woman would have been good enough for Kallie's husband in his mother's eyes. She most likely had a relationship with her son based on an obsession of some sort. It happens more often than you'd think."

"So the mother arranges to get her daughter-in-law fired?" Tj asked. "It seems sort of convoluted."

"Most good mysteries are," Bookman said.

"Maybe, but this isn't one of your books."

"You said Kallie's ex-boss testified on the grandmother's behalf during the custody trial," Bookman pointed out. "Doesn't that make it seem likely he was working for her all along?"

"Why would he do it?" Tj asked.

"Money," Doc proposed.

Tj thought about it. Bookman did have a point. If Kallie's mother-in-law planned to gain custody of her grandson all along, what better way to do so than to create a situation in which Kallie really couldn't care for her child? Once the door was open . . .

"If that's true and the whole thing was a setup from the beginning, how do we prove it?" Tj asked.

"I'm not sure we can," Kyle admitted.

"Or that we should," Ben added. "Did Kallie ask for your help?"

"No," Tj admitted.

"Then perhaps we should let her private life remain private."

"I guess." Tj tossed her cards on the table. "I'm going to get a glass of wine. Would anyone like anything?"

"I could use some of that chocolate cake that's left from dinner. In fact, why don't we take a break and we can all have some?"

"You guys can continue playing. I'll bring the cake to you," Tj offered.

"I'll help you." Kyle tossed his cards on the table and followed Tj into the kitchen. She sliced the cake while he gathered plates.

"I wanted to ask you about a gift for Kiara," Kyle said. "I've asked her many times what she'd like for Christmas, but she refuses to say anything other than that I've already done so much for her and she doesn't need a single thing. Annabeth was very forthcoming with several suggestions about what she might like, but Kiara is about as stubborn as they come."

"Kiara took care of herself for a long time before you started looking after her. I'm sure there's a part of her that doesn't want to lose that independence. Having said that, I know Kiara needs a car."

"I offered to get her one when she started school, but she pointed out that she doesn't have a driver's license and is fine riding the bus."

"Again, she doesn't want to become dependent on you and doesn't want to take advantage of your generosity. I have a feeling that if you happened to end up with a good used car you had no idea what you were going to do with, Kiara might be persuaded to get her license and take if off your hands."

Kyle added forks and napkins to the serving platter. "You think so? I'd really like to get her a new car that she wouldn't have to worry about being dependable."

Tj wiped the chocolate from her hands. "A new car won't work. She'll know it was a gift. But a used car that someone gave you or that you bought from a friend to help him out should do the trick. But you can't make a big deal out of it. You're going to have to convince her that having the car is a hassle you'd just as soon not have. In other words, you'll need to make up a really good story."

Kyle frowned. "I don't know. Kiara is pretty smart. She'll see right through it."

"Of course she will, but that's not the point. You'll know what you're really doing and she'll know what you're really doing, but it will still allow her to accept the gift without feeling like she's taking charity from you."

Kyle chuckled. "That makes no sense."

Tj shrugged as she added cups of coffee to the tray. "It doesn't have to."

"So how am I going to give the car I'm suddenly burdened with to Kiara for Christmas if it's not supposed to be a gift?"

"Oh, you can't. She'll need to take the car as a favor to you."

"Isn't the point of this entire conversation to identify a gift for me to give Kiara on Christmas?"

"That may be where it started, but I guess that isn't where it ended up. Get Kiara clothes for Christmas. I'll help you choose some."

Kyle picked up the serving tray and started back toward the dining table where the others were waiting. "Tj Jensen, you're a devious woman."

Chapter 13

Saturday, December 13

Tj planned to meet Jenna for an afternoon of shopping before the cookie exchange that evening, but first she wanted to stop by the Serenity Motor Inn and have a chat with owner Colin Welsh. Colin had bought the place about ten years earlier and had been an active member of the Serenity Chamber of Commerce ever since. Tj didn't know him very well, but they had served on a couple of committees together and she was acquainted with him enough to know that he was, generally speaking, a reliable guy.

The Motor Inn was located about a mile out of town, perched quite spectacularly on the bank of the Paradise River. In the spring white-water rafters migrated to the Motor Inn, which served as an ideal launching point for daylong float trips through the dense forest. During the off season, however, it was mostly deserted except for weekends, when visitors came to enjoy the solitude of the quaint, isolated facility.

Since it was a Saturday in December, there was a NO VACANCY sign displayed out front. Tj knew that many out-of-town skiers looking for an affordable place to hang their hats when they weren't on the slopes kept the Motor Inn in business during the winter months. While the rooms were functional but really nothing special, Colin had remodeled the lobby to include a cozy fireplace where his patrons could gather for an after-ski cocktail or a cozy afternoon reading in the rustic log structure.

"Tj, what brings you all the way out here?" Colin asked.

While the "all the way out here" wasn't really all that far, Tj rarely had reason to visit the popular establishment. "I wanted to ask you about a visitor you had last summer. I believe he checked in as Rupert Kingston."

Colin smiled. "Once I realized that the man who stayed with me last summer was the same one who died out at the Hideaway, I figured you might be by."

"Why is that?"

"It seems you're developing a local reputation as a freelance investigator."

"I'm not really investigating," Tj said, remembering the borrowed deputy's warning. "But I do have friends on the line, so I guess I'm casually asking around."

Colin laughed. "Whatever way you want to label it is fine by me. The man was a real interesting sort. Not easy to forget." He set aside the ledger he'd been working on. "Most of my guests have headed to the mountain for the day, so I have a few minutes. Would you like a cup of coffee?"

"I would, thank you."

Tj sat down on one of the sofas surrounding the cozy fire. Colin set a cup of hot black coffee on the table in front of her. Christmas music played in the background as the television, which had been muted to provide up-to-date news but not serve as an intrusion, featured a weather report predicting another big storm before the end of the week.

"So about this Rupert Kingston—or I guess I should say Bob King . . . I'm not clear which of the two is his real name."

"To be honest, I don't know his real name either. Kyle indicated that Bob King didn't show up until after Rupert Kingston graduated college, so we're operating under the assumption that Rupert Kingston is his real name and he for some reason created Bob King as an alias later in life."

"Guess you might not want to use your real name when you swindle folks."

"Yeah, I suppose not. Anyway, I was speaking to Nikki Weston, who mentioned that he'd stayed here over the summer. I hoped you might have some insight into the man."

"I didn't speak to him in depth," Colin said. "He checked in late one evening. Normally, I wouldn't have any rooms available without a reservation in August, but I'd had a cancellation, so I told him I could put him up for a few nights. We didn't chat, but he seemed to know some folks in the area, and I got the feeling he might be on the prowl, if you know what I mean."

Tj knew exactly what he meant.

"I saw at least three women either coming or going from his room during his stay. While I have no way of knowing what they were doing there, based on the rumors I've heard about the scoundrel, I'd be willing to guess he invited them to be charmed out of their money. Although," the man paused, "if you want my opinion, none of them seemed the type to be taken in by him."

Tj took a sip of her coffee. It was surprisingly good. She wasn't sure why she assumed it wouldn't be. Perhaps she was getting spoiled by the special blend her dad bought for the resort.

"Do you remember who any of the women were? Tj asked.

"Sure. They were all locals. All single, but none who seem to be the one-night stand type, though Ellen Pomeroy is probably the one most likely to fit the profile of the type of woman Mr. Kingston might be on the prowl for."

Tj knew that Ellen was a hairdresser in her midforties who was newly single after her divorce a year earlier. She had always been a steady sort, but after her husband left her for a twenty-five-year-old yoga instructor, she'd lost thirty pounds, frosted her hair, and begun dating with a vengeance.

"Did you speak to Ellen?" Tj wondered.

"No. She didn't even see me. I was in the room where I keep the cleaning supplies early one morning and saw her sneaking out of his room. Her hair was mussed and she had on a dress and heels—the sort of thing she might have worn to dinner the previous evening."

Tj made a mental note to speak to Ellen. It sounded like Colin was spot-on about the reason she was sneaking out of the room, but any little detail might help to nail the real killer. At least with Ellen she didn't think there was a jealous husband or boyfriend in the mix.

"Who else visited Mr. Kingston while he was here?" Tj asked.

"Libby Wells, although she came by during the day and didn't stay for more than an hour. Still, I guess an hour would be enough."

"Dr. Libby Wells?" Libby was the town pediatrician who had dated Hunter for a while, though as far as she knew they were now just friends. Tj was pretty sure the two hadn't been out since Dylan had left town and Hunter had made it his personal mission to look out for her.

"That would be the one."

"Okay, I'll see if I can have a chat with her. Anyone else?"

"The only other female was Rita Halliwell."

Rita Halliwell was the co-owner of Guns and Roses, a retail establishment that sold both guns and roses. When her father died and left his guns-and-ammo store to his two children equally, Rita had decided that she wanted to use her half of the space to open a flower shop. Her brother continued to sell guns and ammo, so the unusual pairing was created.

"Was Rita here during the day, or did she stay over?" Tj asked.

"I saw her talking to Mr. Kingston around seven in the evening. They chatted at the door for a minute and then they went inside. I'm not certain how long she stayed since I retired to my apartment at about that time. Her car was gone the next morning, and Rita is a real firecracker. I don't see her as the type to be wooed by Mr. Kingston's brand of phony-baloney charm."

Tj had to agree that it seemed unlikely that Rita had had an amorous fling with Bob or Rupert or whoever the man was at that point in time. Rita was a strong, independent sort who wasn't married or in a serious relationship by choice. It didn't fit that she would be a likely target for Bob to focus on. Still, she added Rita to her mental list of people to follow up with.

"You said Rita was the only other woman who visited Mr. Kingston. Were there any men?"

"Just one: David Harris."

David was the local pharmacist, Tj's good friend, and gay. Tj couldn't imagine what David would want with someone like Bob King. She hated to even ask him about it, but she did want to help Bonnie, and if she was going to find the killer, she needed to follow every lead, no matter where it might take her.

"Did anything else you might consider odd or noteworthy happen while the man was here?" Tj asked.

Colin thought about it. "There was a fire in the meadow behind the motel. It was a small one, but we had to evacuate until they put it out. The fire was set intentionally, so the fire crew spoke to everyone to see if anyone had seen anything that might lead to the arsonist."

"And was Mr. Kingston in his room at the time?" Tj wondered.

"I honestly don't remember. I suppose if you can get hold of the official report there would be a list of who was here."

Tj thought Dennis could most likely get the report . . . if he was ever allowed to return to his job.

After finishing her coffee and chatting with Colin about the forecast for the upcoming lodging season, Tj headed back into town. She still had a half hour until she needed to meet Jenna, so she decided to stop by Guns and Roses to see if Rita was free for a few minutes. Tj always enjoyed visiting the Roses side of the establishment. Rita had a knack for presentation and displayed plants, gifts, and scented candles in an inviting manner that changed with the seasons. Since it was only twelve days until Christmas, the displays tended toward red and white flowers arranged with dark green pine and fir branches. As in every shop in town, holiday music was playing in the background.

"Interesting decoration," Tj commented to Brandon Halliwell when she walked in the front door. The large moose head that hung on one wall was dressed in a moose-size elf hat, while the full-size stuffed black bear that normally was in the back of the shop had been moved to the front and dressed in a Santa suit. "Santa and his elf?"

"I try to do my part to contribute to the holiday spirit." Brandon grinned.

"You could get rid of all those dead animals you have lurking around. I know that would greatly contribute to my holiday spirit." Tj never had appreciated Brandon's collection.

"This is a guns-and-ammo shop," he reminded her.

Tj sighed. "Yeah, I know. Rita around?"

"In the back. You can go on through."

Tj walked down the hall to the storage area where Rita kept refrigeration units for the flowers. She found the woman she was looking for standing behind a table arranging red and white carnations into a centerpiece that featured not only evergreen branches but four tall candles.

"Tj, so nice to see you. Do you need some flowers?" Rita asked.

"Actually, I just wanted to chat," Tj said, "although now that I'm here, some fresh flowers would be nice."

"If you decide on the flowers let me know; otherwise, I have a few minutes to chat. What's on your mind?"

Tj watched as Rita expertly wove a red silk ribbon the same color as the angora sweater she was wearing through the display. She was a talented designer, and the flowers really did seem to brighten the cold winter day.

"I guess you heard about the murder we had out at the resort."

Rita frowned. "I did, and if you ask me, it couldn't have happened to a nicer guy."

Ouch. "I take it you knew Bob King?"

Rita stopped what she was doing and looked at Tj. "I didn't really know him so much as I had the distinct displeasure of doing business with him when he was in town last summer, although he was going by the name of Rupert Kingston at the time."

"So the two of you weren't romantically involved?" Tj asked.

"What? *Ew.* Of course we weren't involved. The guy was a total toad. Why would you even suggest such a thing?"

"Don't shoot the messenger; you were seen going into his room at the Motor Inn."

Rita's mouth tightened. "He came into the shop and ordered a very expensive bouquet to be delivered to his room the following day. He seemed very nice and sincerely seemed to want to impress his special girl. I did everything he asked for, even though I had to call around to find a couple of the types of flowers he specifically asked for. When it was delivered, he seemed happy with my effort. He complimented me and gave me a big tip. Then he called the next day and said the bouquet wasn't to his liking and he wanted his money back. I went to his room to try to reason with him. I had a huge investment in the arrangement and the last thing I wanted to do was provide a refund."

"Then what happened?" Tj asked.

"When I got there, he handed me the bouquet. The flowers were completely smashed. It looked like someone had tossed the whole thing on the floor and stomped on it. I told him that since the flowers were damaged I couldn't give him a refund, but he pointed out that I advertised a money-back guarantee, and if I didn't refund the cost of the flowers, he was going to turn me in to the Better Business Bureau. He seemed like a totally different guy from the sweet, somewhat insecure man who had ordered the flowers. In the end I decided it wasn't worth the hassle and refunded his money. He totally killed my profit margin for the week, and yes, I most definitely wanted to kill him. But I didn't, if that's what you're here to ask. Brandon and I were at a cousin's in the valley for Thanksgiving if you want to check."

"That won't be necessary," Tj assured her. "I never thought you killed the man, but I'm trying to help Bonnie, so I'm talking to anyone who might have come into contact with him during either of his visits to town. Do you know who the flowers were for?"

"The scumbag didn't say, and he didn't want to include a card. I got the impression he planned to deliver them personally. I'm assuming the recipient wasn't impressed with his gesture. It really was a shame; I think that might have been one of my most beautiful arrangements. He specifically asked for Casa Blanca lilies to be included. They aren't cheap, and I had to special order them and pay express shipping. What do you think?" Rita stood back, admiring the centerpiece she'd been working on.

"It's beautiful. Do you think I could order some of these for the tables in the Grill when it gets closer to the big day?"

"I can make a smaller version for each table with a single candle. I used carnations on this piece, which is the most economical, but you can do it with roses as well."

"Carnations are perfect. I love the red and white with the greenery. Maybe do red candles for the single-candle pieces. I'll need thirty. How long do they last?"

"At least a week, maybe more, depending on how you care for them. The arrangements come in a tray that holds water so you can keep them moist."

"Okay, then I'd like them to be delivered on the twenty-third. Send an invoice over to bookkeeping. I'll tell my staff to watch for it. Oh, and maybe do another larger arrangement for the dining table in the house with both red and white candles."

"Are you planning another huge meal?" Rita asked.

"Not as large. I know Dad has asked Rosalie, and Grandpa always includes Doc and Bookman. We also have a friend of the family staying with us, so there will be at least nine, but it does seem like the numbers tend to grow as the date gets closer."

"I met that yummy Navy man you have staying out at the resort. He came into the Antiquery when I was having lunch the other day, so Jenna introduced us. What's his deal anyway?"

"Deal?"

"Single? Married? Straight? Gay?"

"As far as I know he's single and straight, but he's also only here for a couple more weeks and then he's back to sea."

"It's a shame. The guy is a babe. I've been too busy to date much lately, but I wouldn't mind waking up to him in my stocking."

By the time Tj finished talking to Rita it was time to meet Jenna. Luckily, Tj had managed to get a lot of her shopping done online, so she didn't have a lot of things to find, but it was tradition for her and Jenna to do a mall trip every Christmas. The mall was located in the valley and required a two-hour drive, but the selection of gift items was infinitely greater than what you could find in Serenity.

"I'm afraid there's going to be a slight change in plans," Jenna informed Tj when she walked through the back door of the Antiquery. "Bonnie called in sick, so I can't leave for another hour at least."

"That's too bad. What's wrong with her?"

"Just a flu. If you ask me, all the stress has been really hard on her. Since we're going to get a late start and we have the cookie exchange this evening, I was hoping we could just do our shopping locally this year and save the drive."

Tj shrugged. "Fine by me. I don't have a lot left to get anyway."

"While I," Jenna sighed, "have a ton."

"Don't worry; I'll help you find what you need."

"I was counting on it. While you're waiting, do you think you can run over to the pharmacy to pick up Bonnie's prescription and then drop it off at her house? It will save us having to do it later."

"I'm happy to. I wanted to say hi to David anyway."

Tj exited the door she had just come through, got back into her 4Runner, and headed back through town.

After buying the pharmacy a few years earlier, David had completely remodeled the place, turning a functional but drab store into an inviting shop with old-fashioned appeal. Metal shelves had been replaced by large pine cabinets, neatly labeled but arranged to remind one of something that might be found in one's home. The old black-and-white-speckled linoleum had been replaced with hardwood floors that made Tj think of a country store in a Norman Rockwell painting. The previously white walls had been papered with a mountainlike print in greens and browns, and swag curtains in similar colors were draped around the old white mini blinds, giving the place a warm, homey feeling.

"Hey, Tj; long time no see," David greeted her when she walked in.

Tj hugged him. "I know; I'm sorry. It's been a busy few months. I'm here for Bonnie's prescription."

David walked behind the counter, removed a key from his pocket, and opened the cabinet where he kept filled prescriptions waiting to be picked up. "How's Bonnie doing? I heard what happened."

"She's hanging in, but it's been hard. I'm sure she hasn't been eating or sleeping like she should, which is most likely why she's sick."

"Stress can be hard on the body," David agreed.

"I understand you met with Bob King when he was in town last summer under the name Rupert Kingston."

"I delivered a prescription to his motel room," David verified. "I suppose you're looking into things on Bonnie's behalf?"

"I'm trying to do what I can. I just feel so bad for the entire Elston family. I was wondering if you could tell me anything that might help me figure out who might have killed him."

"I really didn't speak to him. I received a call from his doctor authorizing a refill on a prescription he'd already been taking. I filled the prescription, but he never came to pick it up, so I decided to deliver it on my way home. I knocked on his motel room door and handed it to him and that was it."

"Can you tell me what kind of medicine you delivered?"

David hesitated. "You know I can't tell you that."

Tj shrugged. "You can't blame a girl for trying."

Chapter 14

"Your tree looks beautiful," Tj told Helen later that evening. She and Jenna had decided to arrive at the cookie exchange early to help Helen in case she had any last-minute chores that needed to be attended to. While Tj's tree was a hodgepodge of homemade and store-bought ornaments in every color of the rainbow, Helen's tree was covered entirely in ornaments in white, pink, and gold.

"Thank you. I do love the holiday season. The house always feels so cozy and inviting with all the lights and the bright colors."

"Your home is always cozy and inviting," Tj added. Helen lived in town, in a two-story house that was more modern than many of the others in the area. As with every aspect of Helen's life, her home was immaculate. She'd taken care to combine the antiques she loved with modern pieces that created an elegant Christmas setting with a Norman Rockwell feel.

"I'm glad you girls came by early. I really could use the help. I took some soup over to Bonnie and ended up staying later than I'd planned."

"How is she feeling?" Tj asked.

"Not great. I think the stress is getting to her. She hasn't been able to sleep since this whole thing happened, and I know she isn't eating the way she should. I'm really worried about her."

"Dennis went by her house earlier in the day to take care of a few chores Bonnie had asked him to handle before Thanksgiving, and he said she just sat staring at the wall the entire time he was there," Jenna added. "He said it was almost like she was in a trance. It really freaked him out. He tried to talk to her about everything, but she refused."

"You don't think Bonnie thinks Dennis . . ." Tj left the thought unfinished.

Jenna frowned. "I wouldn't think so, but if she thinks Dennis did kill Bob, I can see how that would add to her stress level. We really need to figure out who did this so the entire family can get on with our lives."

"We'll get to the bottom of this," Tj promised, "though right now I seem to be hitting dead end after dead end. Still, it's too bad Bonnie won't be able to be here tonight. She always really enjoys the cookie exchange."

"It's a shame," Helen agreed. "She's been working on her cookie for months. But enough about things we can't control: how did you girls do on your shopping trip today?"

"I got almost everything on my list." Jenna beamed. "You haven't already replaced that old blender, have you?"

Helen rolled her eyes. "No, dear. A blender would be a nice surprise."

Tj tried not to smile. She knew Jenna had gotten Helen a beautiful antique quilt that would go perfectly in her house.

"And did you get everything on your list as well?" Helen asked Tj.

"Almost. I just need to find a stocking for Jordan, and something to put into it."

"He's such a nice young man, and so polite. And talk about a rock. He was so kind to the girls and me on the day of the murder. I was on the verge of dissolving into a big puddly mess, but he held everything together."

Tj sincerely doubted Helen was anywhere near a "puddly mess," but it *had* been nice of Jordan to step in and handle things during a time of extreme stress.

"I'd like to get him something as well," Helen said. She furrowed her brow. "How exactly do you know this man? The girls call him Uncle Jordan, but I've never heard of an Uncle Jordan before this visit."

"He was a friend of my mom's." Tj decided to leave it at that. Helen would assume they were good friends and the girls knew him well because he used to visit when she was alive and they were living with her.

"It's nice he could come to visit over the holidays. I'm sure a life at sea gets lonely at times."

"He's on a boat with hundreds of other men and women," Tj said. "I doubt he's ever alone."

"That's not the kind of lonely I meant."

Helen had a point. Jordan had mentioned that he didn't have any family. Maybe he was lonely in spite of his choice of lifestyle. Tj hated to think of anyone being alone in the world. One advantage of having such a large family was that there was always someone there when she needed a shoulder to lean on or a sympathetic ear to listen to her concerns.

"It looks like Harriet just pulled up with Frannie and Hazel," Jenna announced. "I'm anxious to hear how the town meeting went. People have been talking about it all day."

"It was a private meeting," Helen said. "I'm sure Harriet doesn't know how it went."

Jenna laughed. "Yeah right."

Helen smiled. "I guess you're right. She does seem to find a way to know everything there is to know about what goes on in this town."

After Harriet, Frannie, and Hazel had displayed the cookies they'd brought on the dining room table with the others, they settled onto the sofa with cups of eggnog.

"So," Helen began, turning to Harriet, "I wanted to call you today, but I was swamped with Bonnie calling in sick and didn't get the opportunity. How did the meeting go?"

"You realize it was a closed-door meeting?"

"I realize that. Did they decide on a new mayor?"

Harriet sat forward on the sofa. "They discussed someone to speak to, but I'm not sure how that went."

"So spill," Jenna said impatiently.

"They asked Doc, but he declined, and Bookman was also considered, but with his new book he's already swamped. They talked about asking Jake Hanson, but his health has been declining, and of course Hunter is much too busy at the hospital. I know both your dad and grandpa were asked," Harriet looked at Tj, "but both claimed to be too busy with the resort. Hank Hammond's name came up as a possible candidate if they decided to go with a part-time mayor and a full-time town manager. Kyle was considered, but he's new to the town and the council. In the end they decided to speak to Harold Harper."

"Judge Harper?" Helen asked.

"He'd be perfect," Tj realized. "He's lived here forever; he's recently retired so he has an excess of free time; he's still young enough that his health is good, and he's certainly familiar with the idea of setting and upholding the law."

"And everyone already respects him and yields to his opinion," Jenna added. "He really would be a good choice."

"It was actually Kyle's suggestion," Harriet informed them. "I have a feeling that if Harper does accept the position, Kyle will be next in line when he's had a bit more time in the area and experience on the council. Everyone is very impressed by his ability to think on his feet."

"Yeah, he's pretty great," Tj agreed.

"It looks like several cars just pulled up," Frannie announced.

Nikki filed in, followed by Rosalie, Kyle's mom, Vicki Donovan, high-school counselor Sheila Remington, Bren, and Emma Grainger.

"It looks like we're all here now," Helen announced. "Bonnie is still ill, so I guess we'll have an odd number, but I made a second kind of cookie to replace the one Bonnie would have brought, so I'm sure we can work it out."

"If you need a twelfth body, I just left Libby Well's office," Sheila offered. "Dr. Wells offered to meet me on a Saturday to take a look at the congestion the baby has been battling for a few days. I mentioned that I needed to hurry in order to get here on time and she said she'd love to do something like this."

"Call her up," Tj said, jumping right in. No one could say she was one to pass up an opportunity when it presented itself.

Libby Wells was a young, beautiful woman who served as the town's only pediatrician, although in a place as small as Serenity, the local doctors tended to generalize and treat anyone who needed treating.

Rosalie had entertained the Jensen clan on many an occasion with tales of removing a fish hook from a hand or stitching a gash on a leg when the hospital was overrun due to an accident on the highway or an incident at one of the ski resorts. Although she was the only veterinarian in town, there were those who wouldn't hesitate to ask about their gout when they had their dog in for a shot or their cat in for an annual checkup.

Once Libby arrived, the games Helen had planned commenced, so it wasn't until after everyone had gathered to choose and package the cookies they wanted to take home that Tj had a chance to speak to Libby alone.

"Which cookies did you bring?" Libby asked Tj.

"I think the oatmeal, but I'm not sure. Jenna made them for me when I told her I'd planned to bring Oreos."

Libby laughed. "Since I was a last-minute addition to the party I didn't bring anything, but I can assure you that Oreos, or maybe Nutter Butters, would have been my cookie of choice as well."

"I guess as the newest doctor in town you must work a lot of hours," Tj commented.

"I do a lot of shifts as the on-call doctor. It provides me with a little extra income and also earns me goodwill points with the more seasoned doctors who don't want to do it. It can be challenging at times, since I'm a pediatrician, and when I'm on call I'm expected to deal with pretty much anything that comes up."

Tj picked up one of the pieces of bunt cake Helen had served as dessert and took a bite. "I suppose that treating patients outside your area of expertise is common practice in our town."

"It is, and trust me, it's not always easy. I've had plenty of instances when people who really did need treatment decided to wait until the next day, when they could see Hunter or one of the more established doctors."

"I guess it takes quite a few years of treating folks before they begin to believe you know what you're doing."

"Hunter hasn't been a doctor any longer than I have, but he seems to have a reputation in this town that rivals only his grandfather's," Libby said.

"Hunter cut his baby teeth on a stethoscope," Tj commented. "And he grew up not only as Jake Hanson's grandson but as the high-school football hero. He's gold as far as most people are concerned. I think that while Hunter hasn't been a doctor any longer than you have, he's lived here longer. A lot longer. Give it time. Folks will begin to trust you the way they trust him."

"I hope so."

Libby took a sip of her tea as Tj searched for a way to bring up her visit to Rupert Kingston.

"I guess you heard about what happened at the resort over Thanksgiving," Tj finally jumped in.

"If you mean the guy who died, yeah, I heard. Everyone has been talking about it."

"The man visited Serenity in August using the name Rupert Kingston."

Libby frowned. "Why does that name sound familiar?"

"It seems you met him. He stayed at the Serenity Motor Inn when he was here."

"Of course."

"So you remember going to his room?" Tj asked.

"Of course I remember. I have an excellent memory."

"Do you mind telling me why you went there?"

Libby hesitated. "Why do you want to know?"

Tj took a deep breath. She didn't know Libby all that well, so she needed to tread lightly if she was going to gain her confidence.

"You heard Bonnie Elston confessed to killing the man?"

Libby looked surprised. "Bonnie killed someone?"

Did this woman live in a cave? No wonder people didn't trust her. She obviously didn't take the time to keep up with what was going on in the town she served.

"She didn't kill him, but she confessed to doing it in order to get Dennis out of jail."

Libby furrowed her brow. "Who's Dennis?"

"Dennis Elston. Bonnie's son, Jenna's husband, Mr. July on the annual firefighter calendar."

Libby smiled as the pieces fell into place. "Oh, that Dennis. He killed Rupert Kingston?"

"No, but he was charged with killing him."

Libby didn't say anything right away, but Tj could tell by her facial expression that she was beginning to catch on.

"Anyway, I'm trying to help both Bonnie and Dennis by tracking down the real killer. I'm speaking to everyone who might have known the man or even had contact with him."

Libby picked up a carrot stick and nibbled on the end. "Why are *you* looking into it? Don't we have people who do that for a living?"

"Not very well," Tj admitted. "All I need to know is why you went to his room."

Libby shrugged. "It was a Sunday, so I was the only one on call that day. The answering service we use contacted me and told me that a man who was staying at the Motor Inn had called in asking to see a doctor. Normally, I would have had him come to the hospital, but the service told me the man was unable to drive, so I made a house call. When I got to the Motor Inn the man said he was feeling better and didn't need my services. I wanted to be certain he really was okay, so I used the excuse that I needed him to fill out some paperwork since I'd actually responded to the call. He invited me in and I chatted with him for maybe twenty minutes while he filled out the forms, and then I left."

"Did you have any further contact with him?" Tj asked.

"Nope, that was it. I never saw him again."

Chapter 15

Sunday, December 14

Sunday mornings were always busy at the resort, so Tj tried to help out at the reservation counter when she could. Her dad always provided coffee, tea, hot cocoa, and a variety of doughnuts and pastries for his guests to nibble on, should they be required to wait in the oftentimes predictable lines.

"It looks like we're pretty much caught up," Tj said to the desk clerk who worked the Sunday morning shift. "The customer in cabin twelve asked me to stop by, so I'll do that now. I have my cell. Call if you need me."

Tj pulled on her snow boots and heavy coat. Jordan was staying in cabin 12, and she had been stressing over the reason for his request since he'd called her that morning. Everything seemed to be going smoothly. He got along well with the family, the girls loved him, and he'd been able to spend a lot of time with them. Tj wondered if things had gone *too* smoothly.

"Tj, thank you for coming by. Come in." Jordan escorted her into the cabin.

He'd done a wonderful job with decorations. The tree was strung with colored lights and decorated with ornaments the girls had made. There were also sister-created masterpieces on the refrigerator door, as well as crayon drawings on several other unoccupied surfaces. There was a pile of wrapped gifts under the tree that, Tj noticed, bore the names of the resort pets. Jordan and the girls must have gone shopping for Echo and the cats during one of their excursions into town.

"Can I get you something to drink?"

"No, I'm fine," Tj said as she sat down on the sofa in front of the fireplace. She took off her coat; the fire made the small cabin quite warm. "So what's up?"

"I wanted to get Christmas gifts for the girls," Jordan began.

Tj let out the breath she'd been holding. That was it? He wanted to talk about gifts for the girls?

"I was hoping you could help me out," Jordan continued.

"I'd be happy to."

"Each girl gave me a list." Jordan placed papers with at least ten items each on the table in front of her.

Tj realized she was going to have to have a talk with her sisters about the true meaning of Christmas.

"I figured they might have asked for similar items from you, so I wanted to share the list with you before I went shopping. I'd hate to buy duplicates of things you'd already gotten."

Tj picked up the lists and began to read. "Ashley asked you for a television for her room?"

"A flat screen," Jordan confirmed. "Forty-eight inches or larger," he added.

Tj laughed. "I'm so sorry. I don't know where this whole greedy gift thing came from. She already asked me to get her a computer."

"I've only known her a short time, but I gather the girls didn't have much in the way of luxuries when they lived with their mother. It's my guess that Ashley realizes that things have changed and is comfortable enough to want to make up for lost time."

"Maybe," Tj acknowledged. "But asking someone she's known for three weeks to buy her a television is quite a bit over the line. I'll talk to her."

"I don't mind the list. I'd like to buy something nice for each of the girls. I don't have anyone else to buy for, and I find that I'm quite enjoying the opportunity to do so. I just wanted to check with you so that I don't get the girls something you don't want them to have."

"Ashley doesn't need a forty-eight-inch television." Tj continued to look at the list. "She asked you for a sewing machine?"

"She mentioned that Jenna was going to teach both her and her friend Kristi to sew. She wanted her own machine so she could practice."

"I can't even sew a button on a blouse, but Ashley is very creative and seems to have a knack for fashion. If Jenna is going to teach her how to use it, I think a sewing machine would be perfect. There's a corner in her room where we have an old bookshelf, but maybe we can find her a sewing table with drawers to put her supplies in as well."

"I'd love to look for a used one that I can refinish while I'm here," Jordan said.

"Talk to Helen. She's the queen of used anything. And as for Gracie, she's getting her new baby from Santa if Kyle comes through like he promised, so maybe a cradle to put next to her bed would be something special. I'm sure Helen can help you find a used one you could fix up as well."

Jordan smiled. "I love both ideas. I'll call Helen this afternoon."

"Great." Tj began to get up.

"That's not all," Jordan added before she could get all the way to her feet.

"It's not?"

"No. I also wanted to talk to you about Gracie. My relationship with Gracie, to be more exact."

Ah, so the other shoe has dropped. Tj sat back down. "What's on your mind?"

"Since I've been here I've realized how much I've missed not having a family. I fully expected to come to Serenity, meet Gracie, satisfy myself that she was well taken care of, possibly offer a bit of money toward her support, and then be on my way."

"And now?" Tj felt her heart pounding as she waited for his reply.

"Now I find that the past three weeks have been the best of my life. I love Gracie. I don't know that I can simply walk away."

"You aren't going to take her?"

"No," Jordan assured Tj. "I would never do that. I can see how much you love each other. She's happy here with her large extended family. I want that for her. But I also want it for me. My contract with the Navy is up next summer and I'm seriously considering retiring and moving to Serenity. I can't believe I'm even saying that. The Navy has been my life. I've never wanted to do anything else and I really do love it. But what you have here, in this town, with your family . . . I find that I want that as well."

Tj didn't say anything as she struggled to gather her thoughts. If Jordan stayed, would he eventually decide he wanted Gracie to live with him? Would he tire of Serenity and take her away? He'd only been here three weeks and already he'd altered his original plans. Did she really trust him to stick to any agreement he might make about the future? The safest course of action seemed to be to have him away at sea.

"What if it turns out you hate Serenity?" Tj asked. "It's a small town and not a whole lot happens here. You've been all over the world. What if you got bored, but you'd already given up your position with the Navy?"

"I've thought about that, and to be honest, I'm still considering all my options. I realize Serenity offers a specific way of life that isn't for everyone, but if I could be here to watch Gracie grow up, it might be worth any adjustments I might have to make."

"Okay, there is that, but what if Gracie isn't your daughter? We really don't know for sure. What if you give up your career and move here and then find out that she isn't even yours?"

"You make a good point," Jordan acknowledged. "I don't know for certain that Gracie is my daughter, although I feel that if I have the paternity test done and it's negative, I'd still count myself fortunate to be Uncle Jordan to both of your sisters."

"What about a job?" Tj asked. "There isn't a huge call for Navy captains in the area."

"Honestly, I'm not sure what I'll want to do regarding a career if I choose to leave the Navy. I have a degree and I have quite a bit of money saved up. I figure I can work on the specifics once I get here. I'm really good at math; maybe I could get a job as a teacher at the local high school. Or maybe I could open my own business of some sort."

Tj looked out of the window. It was beginning to snow again. She liked Jordan, but as hard as she tried, all she could feel was fear at the idea of him moving into their lives permanently. Not that she could stop him; he certainly didn't need your permission to move to Serenity.

"I know this is sudden," Jordan offered, "and nothing is certain at this point. I just wanted you to know what was on my mind."

"I appreciate that."

"I'm not going to take her from you," he assured Tj again.

She looked him directly in the eye. "I really want to believe that."

"If I move to Serenity—and a lot still has to happen before that can be a reality—I'll move to the area as Uncle Jordan. Nothing more. I promise."

Tj forced a smile. "Okay. Then just let me know what you decide."

"Thank you so much for everything," Kallie said to Tj later that evening when the two were in the kitchen doing the dishes after the family meal. "Brady loves it here, and he loves your sisters. This is going to be the best visit ever."

"I'm happy to help out. I've arranged for the girls' Uncle Jordan to keep an eye on all three of the kids during your shift tomorrow." Tj noticed that Kallie stiffened. "Don't worry. Jordan is good with the kids, and I trust him completely." Tj realized that was true.

"He seems really nice, and Brady did seem taken with him when he came by earlier. I think it's the deep voice. Brady's father had a deep voice, and I know Brady can't really remember him, but I hope a part of him will always remember things about his time with his dad."

"I'm sure he'll always have flashes of memory," Tj assured her. "And you can show him photos and talk about him."

"If I get to spend any time with him." Kallie sighed. "My mother-in-law seems to be getting less and less willing to let me have my days with him. I'm amazed she agreed to this arrangement, but perhaps she didn't want to seem petty when others were involved."

Tj turned on the dishwasher and wiped the counters. She knew she needed to have what was bound to be an uncomfortable conversation with the woman she felt so much empathy for, and now seemed as good a time as any. All the kids were in the den watching a Disney movie with her dad and Rosalie and her grandpa was at the Grill having a drink with Doc and Bookman.

"Echo needs to go out for his evening romp," Tj announced. "Do you want to bundle up and come along with me?"

"I'd love to." Kallie smiled. "Brady seems content for the time being."

After both women had donned coats, snow boots, hats, and gloves, Tj let Echo out the door and the trio headed down the path toward the lake. It was a gorgeous evening. The snow had cleared and the stars shone brightly in the winter sky. The moon was just beginning its ascent and it reflected on the still water.

"I guess you probably heard that I'm looking into Bob King's murder," Tj began.

"I'd heard."

"I realize it isn't my place to investigate, but it seems Sheriff Boggs has really dropped the ball again and I'm trying to find the real killer so Bonnie and Dennis will be off the hook."

"That's completely understandable."

"I've put together a timeline for the day of the murder as best I can and am speaking to everyone who was at Thanksgiving dinner. I'm not accusing you of anything, but I need to ask where you went off to the two times you left the building."

Kallie paled. "You think I killed him?"

"I didn't say that. I'm just trying to put together as complete a picture as I can. I remember you telling me that you were going to help Jenna with dinner after we spoke at the appetizer table, but she told me you never showed up in the kitchen, and then you mentioned you were going to the ladies' room around the time Frannie left, but it was a long time before you came back."

Kallie stopped walking. She stood staring out at the water. "I was trying to hide my dirty little secret, but the truth of the matter is, I was outside smoking."

"I didn't know you smoked."

"I don't. I mean, I didn't." Kallie let out a deep breath. "I smoked when I was younger. After I found out I was pregnant with Brady I stopped. I really thought I'd conquered the addiction, but after my ex-monster-in-law refused to let me see my own son over Thanksgiving, I found myself giving into my craving once again. I'm trying to quit again. I *will* quit again. But on Thanksgiving I'm afraid my willpower was all but gone."

Tj bit her lip as she considered Kallie's confession. "So if you were outside both of the times I mentioned, did you happen to see anything?"

"Like what?"

"It just so happens that both of the times you were missing, Bob King was also missing. The reason I asked you about your movement on that day was because after I realized you were both gone at the same time . . ."

"You thought I might have killed the man."

Tj tried not to look guilty.

Kallie thought about it. "I saw Captain Brown talking to him the first time I went outside, before dinner. They seemed to be arguing, which seemed odd because I didn't think they knew each other. And I saw Frannie speaking to him just before she left. As far as the timing goes, Frannie seems the likely suspect, but she's so nice, I can't imagine why she would off some guy she'd just met, even if he was a rude bastard." Kallie tapped her lip. "I also saw Nikki talking to him after dinner."

Tj frowned. That was odd. In all of the times she'd discussed the murder with Nikki, she'd never mentioned talking to the victim.

"I don't suppose you overheard any of these conversations?"

"No, not really. It did seem that everyone was arguing with the man, though. I didn't want anyone to see me smoking so I didn't hang around where the others might see me, but based on the body language I observed, I'd be willing to bet that he ruffled quite a few feathers during his short stay. If you ask me, the man got what he deserved."

"He might have deserved to die, but neither Bonnie nor Dennis deserves to go to prison for killing him."

Chapter 16

Wednesday, December 17

Tj woke to the sound of absolute silence. Since the girls had moved in with her that almost never happened. She looked around the room to see if she had woken in some alternate universe where five people from three generations didn't all live in the same house. Echo snored quietly next to the bed and Cuervo sat in the windowsill, looking at her with outrage that the sun was high in the sky and his breakfast had yet to be served.

Tj slid out of bed and pulled on her heavy winter robe. She slipped her feet into knee-high slippers and started slowly toward the door. She opened it and listened. Still no sound. Not from down the hall, in the den, or even in the kitchen. She made her way down the stairs, calling out as she traveled from her bedroom on the second floor to the kitchen on the first.

"Anyone here?" she called.

"Mornin', darling," her grandpa greeted her. He was fully dressed and sitting at the kitchen table reading the paper and sipping a cup of coffee.

"Where is everyone?" Tj asked.

"Your dad is over at the lodge and Kallie and Jordan took the kids ice skating. It's almost eleven o'clock. Everyone has been up for hours."

"Eleven? Why didn't anyone wake me?"

Grandpa shrugged. "You seemed to have a restless night, and there wasn't any reason to disturb you."

"You heard me walking around at two a.m.," Tj concluded.

She poured herself a cup of coffee and sat down at the table, which looked out over the lake. It really was a beautiful day. Sunny, with blue, blue skies, and just enough fresh powder to make the landscape look like it was covered in whipped cream.

"I tend to be a light sleeper," Ben answered.

"Kallie isn't working today?" Tj asked.

"She's cooking for the dinner shift in the Grill. Jordan stopped by this morning to say hi to the girls, and they asked if he would take them ice skating. Kallie's little guy wanted to go, so they all went together. I think they plan to have lunch in town, and then Jordan is going to take the girls to play practice. They took extra clothes to change into."

"I guess I'll grab a bite and check in with Leiani." Leiani Pope was the lodge manager.

"I already spoke to her, and she assures me that she's covered. It looks like you, my dear, have the day off. Maybe you should head up to the mountain and take advantage of this phenomenal day."

Tj would have loved to spend the day snowboarding, but there was something else she'd been meaning to do but hadn't found the time for. "I think I might call Ellen to see if she can fit me in for a trim."

"Seems like too nice of a day to waste it getting all dolled up," Grandpa commented.

It really was, but "dolled up" wasn't what Tj had in mind. Tracking down a new clue in a murder case that seemed to be going nowhere would go a long way toward adding meaning to her otherwise delightfully meaningless day.

"I'm so glad you called when you did," Ellen said to Tj later that afternoon. "I've been booked solid with the holiday season, but I just happened to have a cancellation and your hair really does need some attention."

Tj didn't mention that she could care less about spilt ends since she wore it in a long braid most of the time anyway. Luckily, the other hairdresser who shared the space was off for the day, so it was only Ellen and Tj in the small shop on Main Street.

"I've been meaning to come in, but I've been really busy." Tj decided to open with the small talk and meaningless banter portion of their anticipated conversation.

"I can imagine the resort has been packed," Ellen answered politely as she wrapped a cape around Tj's shoulders. "All the snow we've had this year has been nice, but it's really played havoc with the traffic on the highway. I guess you heard about that big pileup over Thanksgiving?"

"I heard there was an accident but didn't ever get all the facts."

"Seven people were injured," Ellen answered. "Should we take some of this length off? Maybe go a bit shorter?"

"No, just a trim," Tj specified. "And I suppose you heard about the murder we had at the resort on Thanksgiving."

Tj realized that her segue to her main reason for being there was just a tad abrupt, but if she knew

Ellen, they could spend the entire hour of her appointment talking about weather and traffic.

Ellen paused for a moment but then continued to snip away at Tj's ends. "I did hear. It's such a shame."

"Did you hear that the guy had different identities?"

Ellen stopped what she was doing and looked at Tj in the mirror. "You know about my dalliance with Rupert Kingston."

"Yeah," Tj admitted. "I do."

"So that's the real reason for this sudden interest in your hair?"

"I did need a trim," Tj defended herself.

Ellen sighed. "What do you want to know?"

Tj looked into the mirror, attempting to make eye contact with Ellen, who was actually standing behind her. "You won't chop off all my hair if I ask the wrong thing, will you?"

Ellen smiled. "I might."

Tj laughed. She could tell Ellen was joking. Or at least she hoped she was joking.

"Colin Welsh told me that he saw you leaving the victim's room when he visited last summer. I'm not judging; I'm just trying to piece together his actions during both of his visits so I can help figure out who might have killed him."

"You think *I* killed him?"

Tj eyed the scissors in Ellen's hand. She wouldn't look good with a bob.

"No, of course not. I just hoped you could give me some insight into the man."

Ellen returned to her trimming. "I know everyone is saying that Rupert Kingston and this Bob King are the same man, but I'm having a hard time reconciling that in my mind. According to the local gossip, this Bob King was a real snake, but the man I met was sweet and considerate and vulnerable."

"Really?"

Ellen was the first person Tj had talked to who had had anything positive to say about the guy.

"Do you mind telling me how you met?" Tj asked.

"We met in the bar down by the river. Do you remember Pat West?"

"The guy you dated a while back?"

"That would be him."

"I hear he moved."

"Pat and I dated for almost a year. I really thought he was the one. We got along great, and he seemed to love me as much as I loved him," Ellen shared. "And then last summer he got a job offer on the East Coast. When he told me that he planned to accept it, I hoped he'd ask me to go with him, but he didn't. The night I hooked up with Rupert was the first time I'd come out of my house since Pat left. I was alone and depressed and he was alone and seemed depressed himself, so we started talking. It turned out that he was in town to try to rekindle things with a woman from his past. He never mentioned a name, but he told me that she had been the love of his life, the one he should never have let get away."

Frannie, Tj realized.

"She'd made it clear that she never wanted to see him again and he was heartbroken. We both were hurting and had a lot to drink, one thing led to another, and . . . well, I guess you know the rest."

"Did you see him after that?" Tj asked.

"No, I never saw him again."

"And once you got back to his room, did he continue to be sweet and vulnerable or did he turn into Mr. Hyde?"

Ellen looked at Tj in the mirror. "He was so sweet and so thoughtful and such a caring lover. When I heard that the man I spent that night with and the man who everyone seemed to love to hate were the same person, I couldn't believe it. I still can't really come to terms with it. The man I was with didn't seem to have a mean or spiteful bone in his body. I don't know who killed Rupert, but I do hope you find them. The man I remember deserves to have justice for his untimely death."

After Tj left Ellen's she headed back toward the library. Something wasn't adding up, and she hoped Frannie could help her make sense of it.

Frannie was busy at the desk, so Tj decided to browse the section that featured new books. There were several cozy mysteries she'd been dying to read, but so far she hadn't found the time to do much more than drool over the colorful book covers.

"Interested in a new cozy?" Frannie asked after the patrons she was helping had left.

"I still haven't read the books I checked out last time I was here," Tj said. "Things have been even busier than normal as of late."

"How are things going with your investigation?"

"Nowhere," Tj admitted. "I did have a couple more questions for you, if you have a moment."

"Certainly, if it will help. Let's have a seat in the back. I'll need to listen for the door, but it's been slow today. Everyone must be busy getting ready for the holiday."

Frannie poured cups of coffee for both of them and then indicated that they should sit down at a small table in the corner of her office. "How can I help you?" Frannie asked.

Tj decided to begin with the question that had been lingering in her mind since her first visit. "I know we've established that Arnie had no motive to kill Bob, but I wanted to ask about his reaction to Rupert showing up and trying to pick up where he left off after he hurt you so deeply."

"He didn't have any reaction because he didn't know anything about Rupert's visit," Frannie explained. "Arnie was out of town at the time, and I never told him Rupert had come to town."

Frannie's answer satisfied Tj that Arnie really didn't have a motive to kill the man.

"I spoke to someone who also knew Bob as Rupert," Tj added. "She indicated that the man she knew was sweet and kind and vulnerable. Does that sound at all like the man you knew?"

Frannie smiled a sad smile. "Actually, it sounds exactly like the man I first fell in love with. He was so sweet and sort of shy. He really cared about my needs and went out of his way to make sure I was cared for and happy. I really thought we had a future."

"So when did you notice a change?" Tj asked.

"It was toward the end of his senior year. He was under a lot of pressure from his family to make a decision about his future, and there were finals to get through and plans to make. He told me that he needed to go home to visit with his parents, but he never came back. It was, of course, devastating for me at the time and, to be honest, it's continued to be difficult for me in the present."

"Difficult in the present?" Tj asked.

"When he came to see me last summer he seemed like the same old Rupert. He was sweet and thoughtful. Part of me was sorry to see him go, but I wasn't up for putting my heart out there to be stomped on again."

"So you stomped on his flowers instead."

"Flowers? What flowers?"

"So let me get this straight," Jenna said later that evening. She was sitting next to Tj in the community center while the kids rehearsed the play, which would open the following Friday and run two nights. Tj had briefly explained Frannie's prior association with Bob, the flowers, and the fact that said flowers had been smashed and then returned. "Bob has two old flames in Serenity?"

"I guess." Tj shrugged. "Rita told me this Rupert bought a very special bouquet for an old flame he really wanted to impress, but Frannie didn't know anything about any flowers. The only explanation is that Bob had yet another old flame to look up."

"What are the odds of that?"

"Pretty astronomical considering he isn't even from here. There's something really odd going on."

"You think?" Jenna asked sarcastically.

"What I find the strangest of all is the inconsistency in the reports of Bob's behavior with the different women I spoke to. How can one man run so hot and cold?"

"I guess it's just part of the role-playing he uses to snare women into his web. He's all sweet and cuddly until he no longer has use for them and then bam: he turns into a monster."

"That does seem to be what's happened. I need to talk to Bonnie. Do you think she's ready to talk about things yet?"

"I don't know." Jenna sighed. "She's made it clear that this whole mess is off limits, but maybe she'd be willing to talk to you."

"I'll give her a call. Maybe I'll even go by tonight. By the way, have you talked to Nikki since she's been gone?"

"No," Jenna said. "Have you?"

"I called her today. Kallie mentioned she saw Nikki talking to Bob the day he died and I wanted to ask her about it."

"Did she know anything?"

"No. She said she went out for some air and he came on to her, which she found disgusting since he was supposed to be engaged to Bonnie. She didn't mention it because she didn't want to hurt Bonnie by saying anything that would imply that the man she was engaged to was a total jerk."

"I guess that makes sense, but you'd think she would have said something after he died."

"Yeah, you'd think. Anyway, the really interesting news is that it looks like she's made a love connection since she's been home."

"Really? With who?"

"Some guy named Joeystein."

"Joeystein?" Jenna laughed. "Have you been dipping into your grandpa's scotch again?"

"The guy's name is actually Joe, but he earned the nickname Joeystein in high school because he was a star football player like Joe Montana and a brainiac like Einstein. Nikki told me she'd had a thing for him a long time ago. Seems they ran into each other and long-suppressed flames reignited."

"'Long-suppressed flames'? Have you been reading romance novels again?"

"Maybe. The point is that I think she really likes this guy. I wouldn't be surprised if she comes home engaged, or at least seriously hooked up."

"But they live in different states," Jenna pointed out.

"Nikki is a teacher. She could probably get a job where this Joe lives."

"Maybe, but it seems to me that if this guy is really into her, he should move to where her job and her life are. I don't see why the girl always has to be the one to move."

Tj was surprised at Jenna's declaration, especially because she tended to be a bit more traditional in her approach to being a wife.

"Something wrong?" Tj asked.

"It's just Dennis. He's been driving me nuts since he's been on leave. He's moody and depressed and constantly underfoot. I need to talk to Captain Brown about letting him go back to work. This murder investigation could take months, and I may have to kill Dennis if I have to deal with his attitude for months."

Chapter 17

Friday, December 19

"How was your day with Jordan yesterday?" Tj asked Kallie. The two had been almost inseparable all week. Tj suspected there might be a romance of sorts going on, but their connection could also have to do with the fact that Jordan had all but taken over caring for Brady when Kallie was at work. Tj had to acknowledge that the guy was popular with all the kids. Maybe he *should* retire from his life at sea and consider settling down to raise a family.

"It was so nice." Kallie got a dreamy look on her face as she sat down across from Tj in the booth in the Grill where she'd been sipping coffee and doing paperwork. "He's such a great guy, and the best thing of all, he almost has my mother-in-law talked into letting me keep Brady for Christmas."

"He spoke to your mother-in-law?"

"He did. On a couple of occasions. Once he found out I wasn't going to get to spend the holiday with my baby he called her up and, in that masterful way of his, demanded that they discuss the situation. Of course I wouldn't expect you to let us stay with you that long. Jordan is willing to watch Brady while I'm at work, so I can go back to my apartment when I'm not working."

Tj smiled. "I'm so happy Jordan was able to make some headway with your mother-in-law, and of course you can stay with us through the holiday if it works out that Brady can stay in Serenity. I realize you chose your apartment based on what you could afford, but it really isn't the best location for a child."

Kallie diverted her eyes. Perhaps she had overstepped, Tj realized.

"I really want to move to a place better suited for Brady when he comes to visit," Kallie explained. "And I know the judge will take my living situation into account when I go back to court to ask for custody. I just haven't been able to find anything in my price range."

"How much do you pay now?" Tj asked.

Kallie mentioned a number.

"Okay, let me check around. I know a lot of people. Maybe someone has an apartment over their garage or a small rental in town. A lot of landlords are willing to take a smaller rent in exchange for having a conscientious renter."

Kallie smiled. "Thanks; that's so nice of you. And I'll let you know about Christmas. I hate to even get my hopes up, but the fact that Jordan is making headway with my monster-in-law is so promising that I can't help but feel hopeful. I didn't get to see Brady at all last Christmas."

"I'm hopeful as well." Tj squeezed Kallie's hand across the table. "If Brady is able to stay, we'll make sure he has the best Christmas ever. And even if he isn't, I want you to come to dinner with the family."

"I'm going to cover dinner in the Grill on Christmas Day so Polly can be with her kids." Polly was one of the Hideaway's full-time chefs. The Grill actually employed four chefs in order to cover all of the days and shifts. Kallie was the restaurant manager but often filled in cooking when one of her staff was off and she couldn't get someone else to cover. "I volunteered when I thought I wasn't going to have Brady and I hate to go back on the offer now."

"Of course," Tj said. "It was nice of you to offer. If Brady stays, we'll work around your schedule. Do you have plans for today?"

"I get off at two. I want to do some shopping; I haven't had a chance to buy Brady's gifts yet. Jordan and I plan to take Brady to the play this evening, and we might go to dinner afterward. I know Jordan was going to talk to you about bringing Ashley and Gracie to dinner as well."

"Actually, Kyle said something about taking the entire cast to Rob's. He rented the back room. You and Jordan should plan to bring Brady. He'll have fun playing with the other kids."

"I'd like that. Thanks for inviting us." Kallie looked at the clock on the wall. "I should get back. The lunch crowd will be coming in at any moment. I'll see you tonight."

After Kallie returned to the kitchen Tj called Kyle to let him know that she'd invited Kallie and Brady to dinner. She also asked him about looking around for a small house for Kallie to rent. He said he'd do some checking and let her know. Tj promised to show up early at the community center to help him set up for his big opening night.

She called Hunter when she got off the phone. He'd left a message earlier that he might have a lead on the letter Jordan had received. Hunter would be at the hospital all day, but if he wasn't actually with a patient he could usually go to his office to take a call.

"Hey, Hunter; I'm calling you back. What'd you find out about the mysterious *A*?"

"The letter was sent to Jordan through a routing center that forwards mail to members of the military who are located in sensitive or secret locations. The letter is read and approved before being forwarded to eliminate the threat of terrorists using the mail as a way to communicate with their operatives. The original return address on the letter was traced back to a woman by the name of Abigail Porter. It seems Abigail and Jordan know each other—or at least they knew each other at one point. It seems she's married to Jordan's college roommate."

The woman must be the love of his life who married his best friend, Tj realized. "How did she know what happened?"

"I don't know. I haven't spoken to her. I figured if Jordan knows this woman he might want to speak to her himself."

"Yeah, you're probably right. I'll track him down and tell him what you found out. And thanks. How *did* you figure this all out?"

"I'd love to take the credit, but Kyle's actually the one who did the backtracking. I asked him to follow up on it after we talked."

Tj smiled. "Don't worry; you still get the credit for following up. It sounds like I owe you both."

"Maybe, and I'd like to cash in on my goodwill credits on a date. A real date. You and me. No kids, no friends, just the two of us. What do you think?"

Tj hesitated.

"If you don't want to I understand."

"I do want to," Tj said, "as long as you realize it's just a date."

"How about tomorrow?"

"That's night two of the play," Tj reminded him.

"Okay, then how about next week? You pick the night."

"Okay. I'll let you know."

"Wow, look at the crowd," Tj said to Kyle and Jenna later that evening. The three of them stood behind the curtain, looking out as they waited for the show to start. Tj could see that Jordan, Kallie, and Brady were sitting with her dad, Rosalie, Ben, Bookman, and Doc. Helen and Bonnie were sitting with Bren, Pastor Dan, and Hannah in the front row, but Dennis was nowhere in sight.

"Where's Dennis?" Tj asked.

"He didn't come. He's really been struggling since he hasn't been working. Captain Brown has been trying to get the county to let him come back, but they're still hesitant."

"This whole thing is ridiculous," Tj sympathized. "Dennis would never kill anyone."

"You and I know that, but the problem is that there wasn't a single person at that dinner who would kill anyone and yet someone did. No matter how you do the math, it still comes up looking like, of the possible choices, Dennis is the only one who makes sense."

"Yeah, I guess I can see that. Still, it really is too bad he didn't come. He'll regret it later when this all gets cleared up."

"I tried to tell him that, but he wouldn't listen," Jenna said. "I thought Jake and Hunter were coming tonight, but I don't see them."

"They are. Grandpa and the guys are saving them seats because Hunter had a last-minute emergency." Tj pointed out two empty seats between Ben and Rosalie.

"I hope the cast doesn't forget their lines," Jenna said nervously. "Standing in front of such a huge crowd has got to put a lot of pressure on a kid."

"They'll do fine," Kyle assured her. "Even if they flub up a bit, the audience is made up of loving parents and grandparents. It'll be fine. By the way," Kyle looked at Tj, "I think I found a little house for Kallie to rent. It's in town near the school and has a huge backyard. There are two bedrooms and a nice, large living area. It's currently for sale, but there's an offer in on it, and I happen to know that if the offer is accepted, the new owner will be willing to rent it to Kallie for what she can afford."

"Are you the potential owner, Kyle?" Tj asked.

"Am I that transparent?"

Tj stood on tiptoe and kissed him on the cheek. "You're a real peach, my friend. Kallie will be thrilled, but I don't think I'll mention it to her until you know for sure that it's going to work out."

"I made the owner an all-cash offer. I don't see any way he won't go for it. I should hear back by the end of the evening, and since it would be all cash, the escrow should go quickly. If Kallie doesn't want it for some reason, it would still a good investment; I should be able to make some money off it if I resell it in a few years."

"You're really getting this rich landowner thing down." Tj was impressed.

"I took a course in real estate investing on the Internet," Kyle admitted. "It's really just common sense, but I picked up some good tips on how to value property. Zachary left me enough money so that I don't need to do anything but sit back and spend it, but I'm too young to take myself out of the game altogether. Besides, the more money I make, the more I can donate, which is something I've found that I very much enjoy doing."

"Well, I for one appreciate your efforts, and I'm sure Kallie will too."

"Hunter just walked in with Jake," Jenna said, "and look who he has with him."

Dennis walked in with Hunter. Everyone scooted down to make room for the unexpected addition. "I wonder how Hunter managed to talk him into coming." Jenna sounded amazed.

"Hunter can be very persuasive," Tj answered. "I'm glad he came. It would have been sad for him to miss the girls' debut."

"Did Jordan tell you how his conversation with the woman who sent the letter went?" Kyle wondered.

"Yes, and thank you for tracking her down. I guess this Abigail felt bad about the way they'd left things years ago. She'd known Jordan had feelings for her, so she knew her engagement to his best friend would hurt him, and she knew he was shipping out the next day. The more she considered the situation, the more certain she was that she might have chosen the wrong friend to marry, so she went to the port to talk to him. She found him in the bar, but he was already talking to my mother. He didn't see her, so she left."

"So if Jordan hadn't been with your mom when Abigail went looking for him, the courses of both their lives might have been altered," Jenna commented.

"Maybe. I suppose if they'd talked and come to the conclusion that they should be together, then yeah, both of their lives might have worked out differently."

"Wow." Jenna sighed.

"Anyway," Tj continued, "several months later Abigail saw my mom in a local store and recognized her. When she realized my mom was pregnant, she went back to the bar and asked the bartender about my mom. My mother was a frequent patron of the bar, so the bartender knew her name and where she lived. He verified that my mom and Jordan had rented one of the rooms in the adjoining motel on the night in question, so Abigail put two and two together."

"So she suspected your mom's baby might belong to Jordan all along?" Jenna asked.

"She did."

"Why did she wait so long to say anything?"

"She didn't know for certain that my mom's baby was Jordan's child, and the bartender told her that my mom was married, so she figured it was best to leave well enough alone. After my mom and her third husband were killed in the auto accident, Abigail happened to see a newspaper article about it. There was a photo of Ashley and Gracie, with a caption that said something about them being orphans, which was actually untrue because it wasn't their father who died with my mom but her new husband. Anyway, when Abigail saw the photo of Gracie she realized Jordan was probably her father."

"So why the secrecy?" Kyle asked. "Why didn't she just tell Jordan what she knew?"

"She admitted to Jordan that she didn't want him to know she'd come to see him that night. It had been years, she was happily married with children, and she assumed he had moved on. She was afraid if he knew that she had reconsidered their relationship, it might affect whatever peace he'd made with the situation."

"Yeah, I can see that." Jenna nodded.

"So she sent the anonymous letter, which led to this point in time," Kyle summed up. "How did Jordan seem after speaking to the woman?"

Tj shrugged. "He's not an easy person to read, but he's been smiling and playing with Brady the whole time we've been talking, so I guess he's okay."

"We should stop chatting and go make sure everyone is ready," Kyle commented.

"The girls have been so excited, I hope everything goes okay," Tj added. "I think I'm more nervous than they are."

"It's going to be great." Kyle put his arm around Tj's shoulder as they walked toward the dressing room.

"Better than great." Jenna looped her arm through Tj's free arm. As the three of them walked toward the dressing room and the cast, Tj realized that there really was nothing better than good friends coming together like a huge extended family.

Chapter 18

Monday, December 22

"Oh my God, I am so excited." Kallie seemed to be about to jump out of her skin with joy as Tj drove her to the house Kyle was in the process of buying. Not only had Kyle managed to get the house for a good price but Jordan had been able to work it out for Brady to stay with his mom until after New Year's, so the boy was going to be able to get a peek at the new house as well.

"Kyle said it's a really great house," Tj confirmed. "And it's close to the school, which will be important because Jordan seems certain he can help you regain custody before Brady starts kindergarten next year."

"Everything is happening so fast. My life had settled into such a dark place, but taking this job, and meeting you and Kyle and Jordan, has made all the difference. I feel like the luckiest girl in the world."

Tj turned from the highway onto a residential street. "I'm glad things seem to be working out. It seems like you were due for some good luck."

"Tell me about it. The past two years have been so hard. Now I feel like my life is beginning all over again. This time I'm going to cherish every moment with my son."

The house was a single story with a large front porch. The front door was centrally located with a large window on either side. Tj knew that based on

Kyle's description, the living room and kitchen/dining area were in the front, while the two bedrooms and shared bath were in the rear.

The house was painted in a soft yellow with white trim around the windows and along the eaves. Snow covered the ground, but Tj knew that beneath the icy surface was a lawn and garden.

"It has a fence all the way around," Kallie commented as she observed the chain-link fence in the front and a tall wooden fence in the rear. "That is so awesome. Brady can play outside and I won't have to worry about him running into the street. I really can't believe I can afford such a nice house. Are you sure you understood Kyle correctly when he told you the rent he was asking for?"

"I'm sure." Tj got out of the vehicle and waited while Kallie unhooked Brady from the car seat in the back. "Kyle got a really good deal on the house and he wants to rent to someone he knows will take care of it."

"I'll treat it like my own," Kallie promised.

Kyle must have heard them pull up because he walked out onto the porch and waved at them to come on in.

"I can't wait to meet the neighbors," Kallie said as they walked up the walkway that someone—probably Kyle—had shoveled. "It looks like the neighbors on the right have kids. Maybe they're young enough for Brady to play with."

"That tricycle looks like it's meant for a child about Brady's age, so maybe they do."

Kallie ran up the steps to the house and hugged Kyle. "Thank you so much. I love it already."

He laughed. "I'm happy to have a renter I know will watch out for the place. Come on inside; you're going to love the kitchen. It's small, but the woman I'm buying the house from loves to cook, so she spared no expense on the appliances."

Tj watched as Kallie made her way through the house, praising every aspect of the cute little home, and Brady ran up and down the hall with the sudden burst of energy that only kids seem to have. The house really was adorable. It would be perfect for Kallie and Brady. Now that Kyle had come through with the house, Tj hoped Jordan could come through with the custody arrangements.

After Tj finished with Kallie she headed to the library to talk to Frannie. It made no sense that Bob had two suitors in Serenity. Maybe she'd misunderstood when Frannie claimed she hadn't received the flowers. Or maybe there was a clue in the timeline of events that she was missing. Tj wasn't sure exactly how understanding the events of the previous summer would help, but her instinct told her to dig a little deeper.

"I'm glad you stopped by," Frannie said when Tj came in the front door of the library. "I've been curious how the investigation is going."

"Not well," Tj admitted. "I'm not getting anywhere, and when I called Roy at home he admitted that they aren't doing any better. It doesn't help that Boggs doesn't consider Bob's death an active investigation because Bonnie confessed. I'm not sure if it will help, but I'd like to understand exactly what happened when Rupert visited last summer."

"Let's have a cup of coffee in the back," Frannie suggested. "I'll hear the door if someone comes in."

Frannie poured two cups of coffee and gestured that Tj should have a seat.

"How can I help you?"

"I know it was months ago, but do you happen to remember what day of the week it was when Rupert came to see you?"

"Actually, I do remember. It was a Friday. I know that because the library is closed on the weekends, and I almost gave into Rupert's charm and agreed to a date on Saturday."

"So he seemed like his old self. The man you remembered from college."

"He really did," Frannie said. "Initially, I told him that I wasn't interested in renewing our relationship, but he managed to talk me into lunch. He was thoughtful and charming and seemed sincere. By the end of the meal I had pretty much convinced myself to accept his invitation for the next day, before I remembered the pain he'd caused, so I turned him down. When he left he said he still loved me and wouldn't give up."

"Did he bring you flowers by any chance?"

"No. I didn't receive any flowers."

"Do you have a favorite flower?" Tj asked. Maybe Rupert had purchased the flowers for Frannie but for some reason had never given them to her.

Frannie thought about it. "I guess my favorite are Casa Blanca lilies."

So he *had* bought the flowers for Frannie, though it seemed he never gave them to her.

"Did you hear from Rupert at all again after your lunch?" Tj asked.

"No. I never saw or heard from him again until Thanksgiving."

"Okay, thanks for sharing this. If I find anything out, I'll let you know."

After Tj left the library she tried to put together everything she'd learned from her inquiries over the past few days. Rupert had visited Frannie on Friday. They'd had lunch. He'd seemed nice and cordial. Ellen had mentioned that she'd spent Friday night with him after Frannie had rejected him. He'd ordered the flowers from Rita on Saturday morning and she'd delivered them that afternoon. The fire had occurred on Saturday night, and Tj had confirmed that Rupert had been at the Motor Inn and had been seen with the crowd, watching the firefighters extinguish the blaze, so he most likely hadn't gone out at all that evening. Libby had seen him on Sunday afternoon, after he'd called the service on Sunday morning, complaining that he didn't feel well, so it didn't seem he'd left the motel on Sunday either. He'd asked Rita for his money back on Monday, so maybe he'd planned to give them to Frannie and then changed his mind. But if he had simply changed his mind, why had they been smashed? Could Bob have done that himself?

David had confirmed that Rupert's doctor had called in a prescription for the man on Monday morning, but Rupert had never picked it up, so David delivered it Monday evening, although Libby had told her that when she saw Rupert on Sunday afternoon he'd said he was fine. Something wasn't adding up.

Later that day Tj met Kyle for drinks at Murphy's. Jenna was tied up, and Tj was trying to keep her distance from Hunter until she'd had a chance to think things through regarding his request for a date, so it was just the two of them. It was only a few days until Christmas and the bar was filled with holiday shoppers scurrying about to find last-minute gifts.

"So where does Bonnie come into this?" Kyle asked after Tj filled him in on everything she'd learned. "Didn't I hear that the reason she went to the cooking retreat was because she met Bob and he invited her?"

"Frannie told me that he noticed Bonnie on Friday, when they'd had lunch. I was able to talk to Bonnie, and she said she met Bob on his way out of town on Tuesday and invited her to the retreat. He was charming and simply lovely—her words," Tj clarified.

"While this is very interesting, I don't see how it helps us."

"I'm not sure," Tj admitted, "but my instinct tells me it's relevant. I'm going to see if I can get Hunter to contact Bob's doctor to find out what he was being treated for. I know there's the whole doctor confidentiality thing, but Hunter's a doctor too, so maybe there's some sort of agreement that doctors can talk to each other."

"Even if Hunter can get Bob's doctor to talk, how is he supposed to find out who this doctor is?" Kyle asked.

"David said Rupert Kingston's doctor called in a prescription. I'm sure Hunter can get the contact info from David."

"Probably. So what's up with you and Hunter?" Kyle abruptly changed the subject.

Tj was shocked Kyle would ask. "What makes you think something is up with me and Hunter?"

"Because I ran into him earlier and mentioned we were meeting for a drink. I asked him if he wanted to join us, and he said you'd been avoiding him so he supposed he should respect your wishes and keep his distance."

"Oh." Tj took a drink of her beer. She really didn't want to talk about Hunter, but Kyle was a good listener and she trusted his opinion, so maybe it couldn't hurt. "Hunter asked me on a date. A real date. You know I love Hunter, but I feel like we're in a good place right now, so I don't want to risk messing that up. Going on a date with Hunter would change things. If it didn't work out I'd lose him. Again. When we broke up it took me a long time to get over it. I just don't think I'm ready to put myself out there like that again."

"Have you told Hunter that?" Kyle asked.

"Not in so many words, but he knows how I feel." Tj looked Kyle in the eye. "I loved him. I was planning my life around marrying him and having his babies. And then, without warning, he came home from college for winter break with some debutante his mom set him up with on his arm."

Kyle took a deep breath but didn't say anything. Tj realized he was probably considering his response. One of the things she loved about him was that when he gave advice he really thought about it beforehand.

"I can tell that Hunter loves you and I don't believe that he would hurt you, but I understand that you've already been hurt. It seems like he's ready to move your relationship from a friendship to something more, but if he's really serious about his feelings for you, it seems to me that he'll wait as long as it takes for you to be ready as well. You should talk to him. Tell him how you feel. If he won't wait, he's not really serious and it's better that you know that now."

Tj hugged Kyle. "Thanks. You always know what to say. I will talk to him. Tomorrow. Right now I'm going to relax with my best friend, or I guess I should say my best friend along with Jenna. I don't want to think about complicated romances or murder investigations that don't seem to be going anywhere. I just want to have a beer and some chicken wings and enjoy the snow and the holiday music."

"You know me. I'm always happy to drink beer and eat chicken wings if it will help out a friend in need."

Chapter 19

Tuesday, December 23

Serenity Community Hospital joined the rest of the town in creating a magical Christmas wonderland. Several fir trees that graced the lawn near the entry had been decked out with white lights, and a large Santa dressed in a lab coat with a stethoscope hanging out of the pocket greeted everyone who entered the lobby. Tj wanted to check in with Hunter regarding the telephone conversation she knew he'd had with Bob King's doctor. He'd told her that he was swamped so she'd offered to bring lunch to him. A quick meal in his office was better than none at all.

"How come your office isn't decorated?" Tj asked Hunter when she came in through the open door.

Hunter looked around. "I guess it didn't occur to me. The rest of the hospital is decorated, and I try not to spend too much time in here, although I find that since my dad retired and moved east, all I do is sit here. Maybe I should have picked up a little tree."

"I'll bring you one of those live trees they have in the grocery store. They're small enough to sit on a table and are already decorated. And when the holiday's over you can plant it in your yard."

Hunter smiled. "Thanks. That would be nice."

"So did you speak to Dr. Livingston?" Tj asked, bringing the conversation around to the real reason for lunch.

"I did."

"Did he tell you anything that will help us figure out who might have killed Bob King?" Tj wondered.

"I'm not sure what I discovered will help us find the killer, but it does explain a lot about the man's behavior." Hunter unwrapped the ham sandwich Tj had brought and took a bite.

"You mean the whole hot-and-cold, good-guy/bad-guy thing?"

"In a nutshell. It seems that Rupert Kingston became Bob King around the time he graduated college."

"We already knew that," Tj reminded Hunter as she began serving the potato salad she'd brought to go with the sandwiches. "We think he changed his name in order to con people."

"He didn't change his name," Hunter clarified. "He *became* Bob King."

Tj frowned. "What do you mean?"

"Rupert Kingston suffered from a condition known as dissociative identity disorder."

"Like the guy in that movie we saw last summer?" Tj asked.

"Sort of. Although it appears that Rupert Kingston had only two personalities, and that the new personality, Bob King, has been in almost total control for most of his life."

Tj furrowed her brow. "What do you mean, 'in charge'?"

"Let me back up. Bob King was in an automobile accident last spring. He suffered from some pretty serious head injuries and spent several weeks in a medically induced coma. When he finally came out of it, he couldn't remember the past thirty or so years of his life, and although his identification said that he was Bob King, he kept insisting he was Rupert Kingston. The hospital staff assigned him to a psychiatrist, Dr. Livingston, because they believed he was suffering from some sort of amnesia."

"Wow, how odd. *Was* he suffering from amnesia?"

"In a way," Hunter answered, "but not for the reason they initially thought. During his therapy sessions the man assigned to Dr. Livingston said he had no idea who Bob King was. He insisted his name was Rupert Kingston. Dr. Livingston did some checking and found out that there actually was a Rupert Kingston and that the man in the hospital fit his description. After a bit of investigation he realized that Rupert Kingston and Bob King were in fact the same person."

"So the man literally became Bob King?" Tj clarified.

"It would seem so."

"Why?"

"Dr. Livingston said he didn't feel right divulging the specifics of Mr. Kingston's personal history. All he would say was that he suffered a personal trauma that seemed to activate the emergence of Bob King. King was a much stronger personality and managed to squelch out Rupert almost completely once he took hold. Rupert did share a few memories with the psychiatrist during which the King personality came to the surface for short periods of time throughout the years, but the memories seemed more like dreams."

"But it was Rupert who came to Serenity last summer," Tj concluded.

"Yes. It was Rupert's identity that awoke from the coma, and he wanted very much to regain the life he'd left behind."

"So he came to Serenity to look up Frannie."

"He did, although it was against Dr. Livingston's advice."

"And what happened?"

"According to Dr. Livingston, Rupert left a long, detailed message on his answering machine during his stay in Serenity, explaining that something had happened that had caused him a great amount of distress and confusion. He claimed he was beginning to experience lapses in memory, which was an indication that Bob was beginning to come through. By the time Dr. Livingston received the message and talked to Rupert that Monday, he suspected it was actually Bob he was speaking to. Dr. Livingston said he went ahead and called David to refill a prescription for the antipsychotic drug Rupert had been taking in the hope that it wasn't too late."

"Rupert must have called Dr. Livingston and left the message on Sunday. When he couldn't get through he must have called the medical hotline, which prompted the service to send Libby to see him."

"That seems to make the most sense. If what Libby says is true, it's probable that Bob was already in charge by the time Libby arrived."

"So it was Rupert who came to town in the first place and it was Rupert who met with Frannie and shared a night with Ellen. And it was Rupert who ordered the flowers, but most likely Bob who returned them, and it must have been Bob who set up the scam to con Bonnie out of her money."

"That would be my guess."

"But it still doesn't explain who killed him."

"No, I'm afraid it doesn't."

Tj headed back into town later that afternoon in response to an SOS from Kyle. She knew he planned to make his Santa deliveries that evening so she wasn't surprised when he'd called in a panic and said he needed some additional help. He'd asked her if he could borrow a second sleigh and also asked if she would be willing to help out as a second elf. Tj wasn't about to dress in green tights, but she did have a pair of green suede pants and a bright red sweater that should do the trick.

"Annabeth, you look adorable," Tj complimented the twelve-year-old elf when she arrived at Kyle's lakefront estate. "I love the costume."

"Thanks. Jenna made it for me. She knew just what I'd want."

"Where's Santa Kyle?" Tj asked.

"Inside, gettin' the rest of the stuff ready. We need to load everything before we can go. You gonna help?"

"I am," Tj verified.

"Kyle went a little present crazy, but I think he has everything organized into groups. We should ask him before we start puttin' stuff in the sleighs."

Tj looked toward the house. "I'll go check with him. Are you waiting for someone?"

It was cold outside, and Annabeth was sitting on the front porch wearing a short elf costume.

"A friend from school. Kyle said she could come with us."

Tj smiled. She was glad Annabeth was making friends. "That's great, but maybe you should wait inside where it's warmer."

Annabeth shrugged. "'K."

Annabeth was right; Kyle really had gone a little present crazy. There were brightly wrapped gifts stacked in piles around the room. At least it did look like he had a method to his madness.

"Good, you're here." Kyle hurried into the room. "I'm afraid I'm running just a bit behind schedule."

"It's going to take you until New Year's to deliver all of this stuff," Tj commented.

"Don't worry; it isn't as bad as it looks. I started with Dan's list and then decided to add gifts for the kids in the play, which made me think about some of the kids in the choir, and one thing led to another. . . ."

Tj laughed. "Preaching to the choir. I brought the second sleigh and wore red and green as requested, but I think the kids are expecting Santa and I'm short one Santa outfit."

"I have a Santa, so I really just needed an extra sleigh and an additional elf."

Tj shrugged. "Okay, I'm game. Who's this mystery Santa I'm going to be spending the evening with?"

"Hunter."

Tj smiled. Suddenly this impromptu assignment seemed like a whole lot more fun.

"Only three houses to go." Tj yawned as she snuggled next to Hunter in the sleigh. Echo sat on the seat behind them. After a bit of consideration Tj had decided he'd make the perfect doggy reindeer, so she'd strapped an antler headband she had onto his head. At first he wasn't thrilled with the accessory, but once they started making deliveries to excited children who wanted to pet him, he quickly forgot he even had it on.

"I have to admit this has been a lot more work than I expected," Hunter commented.

Tj didn't say anything as she allowed the cozy rhythm of the sleigh bells and the warmth provided by the blanket she had wrapped around her body to lull herself into a feeling of contentment.

"When Kyle asked me to do it I was picturing more kissing under the moonlight than lifting and hauling the giant presents he bought," Hunter added. "Do you have any idea what's in those boxes?"

Tj lay her head on Hunter's shoulder. She was enjoying the holiday decorations most houses displayed. Normally, she wouldn't have taken the time to drive around and look at them, but somehow the bright lights and striped candy canes seemed to give Serenity a Christmassy feel that brought a feeling of joy to her soul as they made their way through the quiet streets.

"Actually, I don't know what Kyle bought," Tj answered. "I think there are different gifts for each kid based on what they asked for. Kyle went to a lot of trouble to make sure that everyone's Christmas wish came true."

"I know his asking us to help out went a long way toward making my Christmas wish come true." Hunter leaned his cheek against the top of Tj's head, which was still on his shoulder.

"This really has been fun," Tj agreed.

"Maybe after we finish we can take the sleigh into the woods and . . ." Hunter was cut off by the quacking of his phone. He pulled it out of his pocket and looked at the message. "I need to make a phone call." He handed Tj the reins.

Tj sat up straight and took over as sleigh driver while Hunter spoke to the hospital. Tj could only hear his side of the conversation, but it looked like their trip was going to be cut short by a duck emergency.

"Okay, thanks," Hunter said before hanging up.

He turned and looked at Tj. "Mr. Partridge is complaining of chest pains. An ambulance has been called, but there was a big pileup on the highway going out of town, so all the emergency personnel are tied up. He lives close by, so I'm going to have you drop me at his house. I'll wait with him until the ambulance arrives, which, based on what dispatch told me, should be within half an hour."

"Do you think he's going to be okay?" Tj asked.

"Probably. He's had incidents of chest pains before that turned out to be nothing, but he's getting on in years and I don't want to take any chances. If you want to drop me at his house, maybe you can make the last three deliveries and then come back to get me. Once the ambulance arrives I'll let them take him to the hospital and the doctor on duty can look into it further."

"That sounds fine. He lives on Maple?"

"On the corner of Maple and Elm," Hunter confirmed.

After dropping Hunter at Mr. Partridge's, Tj continued on to the next house on her list. It was starting to snow lightly, and without the warmth from Hunter's body next to hers, she was certain the trips to the last three houses were going to be a lot chillier. Luckily, it was getting late, so the children in each of the three homes had already gone to bed and Tj was able to quickly drop the gifts off with their appreciative parents.

"Looks like that's it," Tj said to Echo, who had moved to the seat next to her once Hunter had vacated the spot.

Echo put a paw on her lap to let her know he was listening to her.

"I guess we'll go and get . . ." Tj heard a loud bang. It seemed to have come from the end of the street, which dead-ended at the edge of the forest. "What the heck was that?" Tj wondered.

Echo barked once. Tj momentarily considered ignoring the sound and returning to Hunter as planned, but some deep-seated instinct caused her to turn the wagon around and head toward the sound. By the time she'd made her way to the solitary house at the end of the lane she could see it was on fire. She reached for her phone, but it wasn't in her pocket. She realized it must have fallen out at some point. She was preparing to rummage around on the floor of the sleigh when Echo jumped down and dashed toward the house.

"Echo, wait," Tj called.

Echo obeyed, stopping immediately, but he began to whine as the flames began shooting from the back of the house.

"Is someone inside?" Tj asked.

Echo barked again.

"Okay, find."

Tj followed Echo into the smoky house. The flames appeared to be the worst in the back bedrooms, but the heat and smoke at the front of the structure was almost intolerable. She was preparing to call Echo off and head back outside when she saw the dog stop and stand over a figure on the floor. Tj took off her sweatshirt and wrapped it around her nose and mouth. She tried to hold her breath as she made her way along the smoky floor toward the man she realized, as she neared, was none other than Captain Brown. He didn't appear to be injured, and it was odd that a trained firefighter would so easily succumb to smoke.

And then she noticed the bottle of tequila. The empty bottle of tequila. Was the man drunk?

Tj grabbed his arm and began to pull him toward the front of the house and the open door. Echo grabbed onto the sleeve on his other arm and pulled as well. Captain Brown was a big man and not easily moved, but Tj was able to make enough progress that she felt she'd be able to rescue the man until there was a loud explosion and everything went dark.

"What happened?" Tj asked as she squinted against the bright light that was causing her eyes to water. She was lying on the snow. Hunter was sitting next to her, shining a light into her eyes.

"You were hit by falling debris and knocked out."

"Debris?" Tj choked as she tried to get her bearings. There was chaos all around her. Red and white lights flashed as men ran around with hoses, attempting to contain the flames that engulfed the house. It was loud, so loud as the fire raged and the men yelled back and forth to one another.

"You went into the fire at Captain Brown's to try to save him. Something fell and hit you on the head and you blacked out. Luckily, Echo pulled you outside. By the time emergency personnel arrived you were lying on the snow."

"Echo—" Tj tried to sit up.

"Is fine," Hunter assured her. "He was in super-protective mode when everyone arrived, so Josh put him onto one of the trucks."

"And the horses?"

"Moved down the road a bit. We've called your dad to come get them."

"I need to get up. I'm sure Echo is frantic." Tj grimaced against the pain in her head as she sat up.

Hunter waved at someone and within seconds Echo came running up. He lay down next to Tj and she wrapped her arms around his large neck and gave him a hug. "Thank you, buddy," she cried into his fur. She realized that if not for her dog she would most likely be dead.

"How long have I been out?" Tj asked.

"Not long. A few minutes."

"How did everyone get here so fast?"

"A neighbor had called in the fire, so the trucks were already on the way when you went inside. I happened to call the hospital to check on the ambulance for Mr. Partridge and they told me about the emergency call. I was close, so I came over. When I got here Josh was wrestling Echo into the truck because he wouldn't let the others near you. I figured the truck was the safest place for him, so I helped Josh get him inside and then I checked on both you and Captain Brown."

"Captain Brown. Is he okay?" Tj looked frantically around the snow-covered ground.

Hunter hesitated. He looked at Tj with sadness in his eyes. "I'm afraid he didn't make it."

Tj closed her eyes. She buried her face in Echo's furry neck and let her sorrow for the man wash over her. Dennis was going to be devastated. He looked up to him like some sort of surrogate father.

"I tried to get him out." Tj sighed as tears streamed down her face.

"It was already too late. He was dead before the fire even started."

Tj frowned. "Do they know what happened?"

"We can talk about that later. Right now I want to get you to the hospital."

"Don't be ridiculous. I'm not going to the hospital. What do you mean, Captain Brown was dead before the fire started? It looked like he was passed out drunk."

"He had been drinking," Hunter confirmed, "but he'd also hit his head. It looked like he'd stumbled around, knocking into things for a bit, before falling and hitting his head on the coffee table. If he drank that whole bottle of tequila it's no wonder he passed out. We really should take you to the hospital to get you checked out."

"I'm not going to the hospital."

"Okay then, at least let's move to one of the police cars. We can wait inside until your dad arrives with the truck."

"Okay." Tj moved onto her knees and then onto her feet. She was a little dizzy and the pain in her head was explosive, but she figured she would survive. Echo sat at her side, the ever-protective watchdog just daring anyone to mess with her. It was a miracle Josh had managed to get him into the truck when she was obviously vulnerable, but Echo was well trained and he knew Josh.

Hunter helped Tj to Roy's car while Echo trotted along at her side. The trio climbed into the backseat where they could wait out of the way of the emergency personnel. Tj wrapped her arms around Hunter's neck and let the tears she'd been fighting flow freely.

Chapter 20

December 24

Christmas Eve was a magical day in the Jensen household and Tj wasn't going to let the events of the previous evening destroy even one minute of the joy she felt being with her family and friends. As he did the day before every Christmas, Ben made a huge breakfast that every family member made a point of attending and enjoying, no matter how busy they might be. This year Jordan, Kallie, and Brady joined the Jensens as they shared plans for the next twenty-four hours.

"I want Papa to read 'The Night Before Christmas' to us like he did last year," Gracie announced.

"I think I can do that." Mike smiled at her.

"And the angel book," Ashley joined in. "Someone has to read the angel book."

"Grandpa can do it," Tj suggested.

"But Grandpa always reads the passage in the Bible about the first Christmas," Ashley pointed out. "Why don't you do it?"

"I'd be happy to, but last year you complained I didn't do it right."

"That's 'cause you have to use the voices."

"Uncle Jordan should do it," Gracie said. She turned and looked at him. "Do you want to?"

Jordan looked at Tj for guidance. She smiled at him. "I'd love to," he said, "but I might need your help with the voices. I don't believe I've heard the story before."

"I can help you." Gracie grinned. "Can we leave out cookies and carrots like we did last year?" she added, turning her attention to Tj.

"Absolutely. And a tall glass of milk as well. Do you have any special Christmas Eve traditions you'd like to share with Brady?" Tj asked Kallie.

She hesitated. "It's your Christmas."

"Nonsense, it's *our* Christmas."

"Well . . ." She hesitated. "Brady's father was brought up Catholic and he always liked to light the advent wreath on Christmas Eve. We'd say a prayer of thanks and then sing some carols."

"That sounds wonderful. Do you have a wreath?"

"No," Kallie said, "but I can go into town and get one."

"Actually, I think there's one upstairs in your grandma's stuff," Ben offered. "Is it round with four candles?"

"It is." Kallie smiled.

Tj took a bite of the delicious muffins Ben had made fresh that morning. She watched as her large extended family laughed and talked among themselves. There really was nothing better than being with family at Christmas.

"Can Kristi and Kari come over later?" Ashley asked once the conversation about favorite traditions died down.

"I invited the whole Elston family to come over," Tj answered. "They're going to be here all day and then stay for dinner."

"I insist that you let me do the cooking," Kallie spoke up. "You're supposed to be taking it easy.

Besides, I really want to do something nice to thank you for everything you've done for Brady and me."

"It's okay with me," Tj said, looking at Ben.

"Fine by me. I invited the guys to come for dinner, so if Kallie cooks it will free me up to play some cards."

"I've invited Rosalie as well," Mike joined in.

"I guess I'd better get in the kitchen." Kallie seemed really excited about the opportunity to contribute, but she frowned when she realized that Brady would be left on his own.

"I'll take the kids out to burn off some steam," Jordan offered. "I've been thinking that we need to add a new snowman to our family on the front lawn."

Tj noticed the look of adoration Kallie sent in Jordan's direction. She only hoped her feelings were returned.

After breakfast Mike went to check on the staff while Ben went upstairs to wrap a few last-minute gifts and Tj volunteered to deal with the dishes. Kallie went into town to gather a few special ingredients for the dinner she was enthusiastically planning, while Jordan took the kids outside to build the snowman he'd promised. After she'd finished wiping the counters, Tj poured herself a cup of coffee and sat down at the table to consider her options for the remainder of the day.

"Brady wants to have some hot cocoa." Gracie came inside and slipped onto Tj's lap. "He's cold from the snowman."

"I think that can be arranged."

Gracie bit her lip as she appeared to be trying to work something out in her six-year-old mind. "Is Brady our new brother?" she asked.

Tj laughed. "No, he's just staying with us for a few more days and then he's going back to his grandmother's."

"Why?"

Good question.

"He's staying with his grandma for a while so that his mom can get settled into her new house."

Gracie seemed to consider that. "Where's his daddy?"

"I'm afraid he passed away."

"Like Mom?"

"Yeah, like Mom."

Gracie seemed content with Tj's answers. She wrapped her arms around her sister's neck and snuggled her curly head into her chest. Tj wrapped her arms around the sister she had grown to love so much over the past year and a half, offering a prayer of thanks that she was allowed to have her sisters in her life.

"I think Uncle Jordan likes Kallie," Gracie whispered into Tj's ear.

"You think so?" she whispered back.

"He keeps looking at her and smiling. Uncle Hunter looks at you and smiles, and Grandpa told me it was because he likes you."

Tj smiled. "Uncle Jordan and Kallie are just friends, like Uncle Hunter and I are friends."

"Ashley said you and Uncle Hunter are going to get married as soon as you come to your senses."

Tj laughed. "Ashley said that? Where did she ever get that idea?"

Gracie shrugged. "If you do marry Uncle Hunter, are you still going to live here with me and Ashley?"

Tj hugged Gracie. "I'm not going to marry Uncle Hunter or anyone else any time soon, but even if I do get married someday, you and Ash are my number-one priority. I'll always live with you until you're old enough to move out and live on your own."

Gracie settled her head against Tj's chest as she looked out the window at the others. Tj wrapped her arms around her as they enjoyed the contentment that comes with having those you love most happy and together.

Later that afternoon Tj sat on the front deck with Jenna, watching the kids play in the snow.

"How are you feeling?" Jenna asked. "Perhaps we shouldn't have all descended on you after your ordeal."

"I feel okay," Tj answered. "It seems like Bonnie is doing better today. She's been in the kitchen helping Kallie since she got here. She still looks pale and thin, but her smile seems to be back."

Tj waved to Ashley, who was trying to get her attention so that she would watch her sled down the hill they'd built near the side of the yard. It was a short but steep ride, and all the kids seemed to be having a blast.

"She *is* doing better," Jenna said. "Mom talked to her for quite a while this morning, and it seems like she's ready to put this whole thing behind her. I'm not sure she'll be dating any time soon, but maybe that's just as well."

"Speaking of dating," Tj leaned in close, "did you see the shy looks being exchanged between your mom and Bookman? I know they've been attracted to each other for a while, but I get the feeling there may be more going on."

"Mom is keeping mum about the whole thing, but I'm fairly certain the two have shared a few dates in the past month. If I had to guess I'd say Bookman could be my new daddy."

"And how do you feel about that?" Tj laughed.

"I love the idea. I've known Bookman long enough to have a deep respect for him. He's kind and loyal, and he cares about his friends. And honestly, I think he's one of the few men who would be able to maintain an equal hand with Mom. Most of the men she's dated in the past were so awed by her that they treated her like she was the queen of the town. I know Bookman respects Mom, but he can hold his own with her. I'd hate to see Mom end up with someone she could walk all over."

Tj had to agree that Helen and Bookman made a fine pair. She supposed they'd have to wait to see how everything turned out.

"How's Dennis doing with everything that's happened?" Tj asked.

"It's hard to tell," Jenna said. "On one hand, he's devastated by what happened to Captain Brown, but on the other, he's glad that neither he nor Bonnie is considered a suspect. I think he's anxious to put this all behind him. I know he's grateful to your super dog for rescuing you from a fiery death, as am I."

Tj wrapped her arms around her giant dog and gave him a hug. This wasn't the first time she was glad he'd been trained in search and rescue, and she was sure it wouldn't be the last.

"Has Dennis heard whether he's going to be able to go back to work?" Tj asked.

"Yes, thank goodness. His first day back is the twenty-sixth. I love my husband, but he's been driving me crazy while he's been off. I'll be very happy to have the house to myself for a few hours a day again. Still, I know the entire crew is reeling from what happened. It's going to be a tough adjustment."

It turned out that Captain Brown had sent an e-mail to Deputy Fisher and each of his men a short while before the explosion that ignited the fire. The letter stated that he was directly responsible for Bob King's death and, while he had no desire to live out his life in prison, he also found that he could no longer live with the guilt, no matter how justified he believed his actions might have been, so he planned to commit suicide. It turned out that the pregnant woman Bob King had killed in the hit-and-run accident was Captain Brown's sister. The arresting officer had been new and had made an error, so even though Bob was obviously guilty of killing the woman, he had been release after serving only a few short weeks behind bars.

"Dennis said the e-mail indicated that Captain Brown ran into Bob King when he was in town using the name Rupert Kingston last summer," Jenna informed Tj. "The captain said Bob acted like he didn't even remember killing his sister, and he'd been letting his hatred and resentment fester ever since. He must have snapped when he saw him again."

"I remember wondering at the time I found out about the fire at the Motor Inn last summer if there was a link between Bob's reemergence and the fire," Tj commented. "It didn't seem likely, but if Captain

Brown was the one who talked to Rupert after the fire, he must have known who he was. Rupert wouldn't have remembered the event, but what if Captain Brown reminded him about what happened? It seems like that might have been a traumatic enough experience to serve as the catalyst for Bob to reemerge and regain control."

"Your theory makes sense. It would be pretty awful to find out that you had been a monster during the years you couldn't remember."

"There's one thing that's been nagging at me about the whole thing," Tj added.

"What's that?"

"The fact that the whole thing makes no sense. The story everyone is going with is that Captain Brown got drunk, sent an e-mail to his men that he was guilty of the murder, then committed suicide. Hunter said he actually died as a result of hitting his head, probably while stumbling around the house. Falling and hitting your head isn't committing suicide."

"Maybe he intended to commit suicide but fell and hit his head before he had the opportunity to do so," Jenna speculated.

"Okay then, why the fire? It doesn't seem like Captain Brown would intentionally set a fire. He spent a good part of his life putting out fires, and even with the snow, he had to have known that a house fire always has the potential of spreading to the forest surrounding it."

"You have a good point," Jenna admitted. "It does seem that Captain Brown would use some other method besides fire to end his life, no matter how deeply entrenched in guilt he might be."

"I didn't have a chance to really look around when I was there last night because it was hot and smoky and I just wanted to get the heck out of there, but it did seem like the furnishings had been disturbed. What if someone else was there? Maybe there was a struggle, Captain Brown fell and hit his head, and this other person started the fire to cover things up?"

"You think someone killed Captain Brown and faked the suicide note?" Jenna asked.

"Maybe. Or maybe Captain Brown did send the note with the intention of killing himself, but someone showed up and tried to stop him. There was a struggle and Captain Brown fell and hit his head. The other person panicked and started the fire. We have to go back."

"Back?"

"To the house. I need to look around. I have the feeling there's something I can't quite remember. Something significant."

"Maybe we should tell Dennis or call Roy," Jenna suggested.

"No, not until I can look around on my own. Coming?"

"Well, I'm sure as heck not letting you go alone." Jenna offered to drive since Tj really wasn't supposed to be exerting herself in any way.

The house had been burned badly enough that it would most likely need to be torn down. It seemed obvious that some type of accelerant had been used to make the fire burn hot and fast. Jenna and Tj carefully made their way into the structure, which had been blocked off with yellow caution tape.

"If we aren't careful we're both going to end up in jail," Jenna complained.

"Don't worry. We'll only be here for a minute."

"What exactly are you looking for?"

"Honestly, I'm not sure."

Tj wandered over to the spot where she'd found the body. It was hard to tell whether the disruption to the furniture and decor was due to a struggle before the fire or if it had been the result of the firefighters trying to extinguish the blaze. Captain Brown's computer still sat on his desk. It had been damaged by the heat and water but was basically intact. Tj opened the top desk drawer and gasped.

"I think we need to call Roy," she stated.

"Why? What did you find?" Jenna asked as she walked over to where Tj was looking at a photo.

"Well, I'll be. Maybe there *is* more to this story."

"It was really nice of you to let us all descend on your Christmas Eve dinner." Kyle walked up behind Tj and put his arms around her later that day.

"I'm thrilled to have you," Tj assured him. "Did you bring the doll and computer?"

"I gave them to your dad. He said he'd stash them away until it's time for Santa to make his visit."

"Where is my father?" Tj asked.

"Playing poker with your grandfather and the guys. It seems you've had quite a day. Everyone is talking about the fact that it was really Arnie who killed Bob King. Care to fill me in?"

Certainly. Let's get a drink and head out onto the sun porch. We have quite the crowd, but I don't think anyone is out there at the moment."

Kyle followed Tj to the porch, which was enclosed in glass, offering an excellent view of the lake on a cold winter day.

"So what happened?" Kyle asked after they were both seated.

"Jenna and I were talking earlier and it just didn't make sense to me that Captain Brown would send a suicide note and then die as a result of an accident. It also didn't make sense that he would set his own house on fire. We decided to go back to the house and look around. We found a photo of Captain Brown, a woman who turned out to be his sister and was the woman Bob King killed in the hit-and-run accident, and Arnie. It turned out Arnie was Captain Brown's brother-in-law. It seems the reason Arnie moved to Serenity was because he fell in love with the place when he came to visit Captain Brown. When Arnie saw Bob at the Thanksgiving dinner he freaked. The two men got into a fight, and Arnie ended up hitting Bob with the back of a shovel he'd pulled from the fire truck Captain Brown had brought to the resort. The captain saw the whole thing. He felt bad for Arnie, so the men moved the body away from the truck and left. By the time I stumbled across the body they were long gone."

"But Captain Brown couldn't live with the guilt?" Kyle guessed.

"Arnie confessed that Captain Brown wanted to come clean to the cops about what had happened. He could see how the whole thing was tearing Dennis apart. Arnie panicked and the men, both of whom had been drinking heavily, got into a scuffle. Captain Brown fell and hit his head. Once Arnie realized the captain was dead he sent the e-mail from his computer confessing to killing Bob King and then set the house on fire to cover up any evidence as to what had really happened."

"So Arnie is in jail?"

Tj nodded. "I suppose it will be a long time until he's able to enjoy Christmas on the outside. It's really a shame. Bob killed his wife and unborn child and then got off scot-free. It's understandable that he could become so enraged as to hit him with the shovel. It really does seem like he was a perfectly nice guy who got caught up in circumstances he couldn't control."

"I really hate it when the bad guy ends up being a good guy," Kyle agreed.

"When I realized what must have happened there was a split second when I considered destroying the photo rather than calling Roy."

"I'm sorry to interrupt." Kallie walked out onto the sun porch from the kitchen. "I was wondering how many place settings we needed."

Tj did a quick calculation in her head. "Twenty-three, I think. We might need to bring in the card table and chairs." Tj started to get up.

"You sit; I'll get them," Kyle offered.

Tj and Hunter sat side by side as the horse-drawn sleigh made its way through the silent night. After all the guests had left and the resident kids had been bathed and put to bed, Hunter came back with a bottle of wine, a warm blanket, and an offer to take Tj to a place where the only noise was the sound of their breath in the heavy night air.

"This is so nice." Tj rested her head on Hunter's arm. "I really enjoyed having everyone over, but this is the first time I've had any peace and quiet all day."

"We never did have our date, so I never had a chance to give you your present," Hunter commented.

"You got me a present?"

"It's on the backseat."

Hunter pulled gently on the reins, instructing the horses to stop. He turned around and put a gift-wrapped box in Tj's hand.

"Hunter, you shouldn't have. Really."

"Don't worry; I'm not violating the friends-only dictate we seem to be adhering to. It's just a small gift, not an engagement ring. Open it."

Tj slowly tore open the meticulously wrapped gift. Her heart skipped a beat when she opened the box. "You kept it all this time?"

Lying within the layers of tissue paper was the elf hat she'd worn the first night she and Hunter had gotten together and become a couple.

"Of course I kept it. I was supposed to wear it at our wedding. We had a bet," Hunter reminded her.

Tj laughed as a tear slid down her cheek.

"I'm not giving this to you now because I intend to go back on my commitment to wear the darn thing. When we do eventually marry I plan to wear it proudly. I'm giving it to you because I want you to know that, in spite of everything, I never gave up on us. I was young and stupid and let my mom intimidate me. I can't change that, but I *can* try to convince you that I love you and have loved you since the night you sat on my knee and gave Santa a kiss."

Tj looked up at Hunter. She wanted to speak but found she couldn't.

"I want us to have another chance," Hunter continued. "I'm not asking for a commitment you might not be ready to make. I just want to take you on a date. A real date, and if that goes well, maybe we can have a second and a third date."

Tj threw her arms around Hunter's neck. She still couldn't speak, but in that moment words didn't seem necessary. Hunter had always known how to speak to her heart. A diamond bracelet or an expensive pair of earrings wouldn't have touched her the way this very meaningful gift had.

"Does that mean yes?" Hunter asked as he held her.

Tj pulled back slightly. She lay her hand on Hunter's cheek before she leaned in slowly and kissed the man who had dominated her dreams since the moment they'd shared that first kiss under the stars on that snowy December day all those years ago.

Books by Kathi Daley

Buy them on Amazon today.

Paradise Lake Series:

Pumpkins in Paradise
Snowmen in Paradise
Bikinis in Paradise
Christmas in Paradise
Puppies in Paradise – *February 2015*

Zoe Donovan Mysteries:

Halloween Hijinks
The Trouble With Turkeys
Christmas Crazy
Cupid's Curse
Big Bunny Bump-off
Beach Blanket Barbie
Maui Madness
Derby Divas
Haunted Hamlet
Halloween Hijinks Anniversary Edition – *September 2014*
Turkeys, Tuxes, and Tabbies – *October 2014*
Christmas Cozy – *November 2014*
Alaskan Alliance – *December 2014*

Road to Christmas Romance:

Road to Christmas Past

Kathi Daley lives with her husband, kids, grandkids, and Bernese mountain dogs in beautiful Lake Tahoe. When she isn't writing, she likes to read (preferably at the beach or by the fire), cook (preferably something with chocolate or cheese), and garden (planting and planning, not weeding). She also enjoys spending time on the water when she's not hiking, biking, or snowshoeing the miles of desolate trails surrounding her home.

Kathi uses the mountain setting in which she lives, along with the animals (wild and domestic) that share her home, as inspiration for her cozy mysteries.

Stay up to date with her newsletter, *The Daley Weekly*. There's a link to sign up on both her Facebook page and her website, or you can access the sign-in sheet at: http://eepurl.com/NRPDf

Visit Kathi:
Facebook at Kathi Daley Books, www.facebook.com/kathidaleybooks
Twitter at Kathi Daley@kathidaley
Webpage www.kathidaley.com
E-mail kathidaley@kathidaley.com

ß0

15998703R00136

Made in the USA
Middletown, DE
02 December 2014